FESTIVAL

FESTIVAL

Chris Tomasini

CreateSpace. Kindle Direct Publishing, 2015.

New edition with new cover, July 2022.

Cover photograph taken September 1, 2021, by Emilia R. Peters, and used with permission by the author.

Festival / by Chris Tomasini.
1. Toronto (Ont.) – Fiction.
2. London – Fiction.

DEDICATION

To those who were in London and
Toronto living this life with me.

PROLOGUE

September 20

Peter:

I hope your parents forward this to you, and you get it before Christmas at least. I kind of feel like I'm putting a message in a bottle, tossing the bottle into the Atlantic, and hoping vaguely that you'll get it. Ah well – me and my eclectic mind.

So you're back in Canada! How was your flight? How was your time in your hometown? How was the move back to Toronto? Any interesting stories to tell? I'd kill for a good story. I'd kill for a story that kept me on the edge of my mental seat with nothing else on earth but the desire to hear the story come to it's conclusion and unfold in a way that took me along some intensely emotional roller-coaster ride that left me shocked for weeks, locked into the images, the characters, a door opened to reveal the world. *Boy is she ever bored!* he whispers upon reading this, well, maybe.

Anyway, September in London has been September in London. It's been cloudy but I've been able to spend a few afternoons dozing in the sun by the Serpentide. The underground and the sidewalks are less clogged, I guess most of the tourists have gone home. The porter they hired to replace you is British. He's nice and everything, and he's gone with us when a bunch of us from the hotel go out, but he doesn't run around causing trouble the way you did. Ruth misses you. I guess the other maids do too, but Ruth hears your name, smiles that bright smile of hers, and tells another story about how much aggravation you caused her. Ferness and Phillips don't miss you of course.

PROLOGUE

I'm thinking of moving to the continent before too long. Come this January I'll have been here a year and I don't really want to stumble through another London winter. It sucks royally here in winter. It's rainy raw and cold, and the English get even paler than they are in the summer.

I've decided that it is absolutely essential to my sense of accomplishment and peace of mind that I become fluent in another language. I've decided French is my best and quickest bet, and living in France or Switzerland would be extremely interesting. Maybe later I will live in Japan for a year then spend a year or more travelling in Australia. (You're probably saying *I don't give a f*&k what she plans on doing* but I thought I would use this letter as a way to start committing myself to this plan. Once it is in writing it is harder to go back on).

In other news I've decided to give up alcohol. I haven't woken up naked on top of a bus or anything, I'm just hoping to prove to myself that I can enjoy life and participate in social events and fun weekends without using alcohol to distort reality and then have to pay for it without dehabilitating hangovers.

In my new fully conscious pseudo-intellectual state I've come across something relevant to what we were talking about when we last saw each other. It's a quote from <u>Even Cowgirls Get the Blues</u>, the main character of which is Sissy Hankshaw, who has monstrously large thumbs which she uses to hitchhike back and forth throughout the USA. Someone asks her what all her travels have proven and she says "I've proven that people aren't trees, so it is false when they speak of roots."

There are some other interesting things said in conjunction with this quote, but I'll leave that to you and any natural curiousity to investigate further. At any rate it is something to ruminate over.

Well, time to wrap things up and bid you adios. I sincerely hope all is working out for you in Toronto. Hope you've found a job and that it and school are not unbearable (I won't say "enjoyable" because I know in your case it's too much to ask. By the way, take a look at "Joie de Vivre" by Matisse in an art book, might cheer away some of your foul humors).

FESTIVAL

    I apologize for the semi-mundanity of this letter but sometimes inspiration forgets to give you a wedgie and life and your so-called creative juices just seem to falter. At any rate, I hope you get the picture.

    Hasta Luego

Anne
London, U.K.

P.S. WHEN you write ME send the letter to my parents' house. I'm not sure how much longer I'll be here.

PART ONE

She prays now, she says, that I may learn in my own life and away from home and friends what the heart is and what it feels.
Amen.

James Joyce
A Portrait of the Artist as a Young Man

TORONTO

I fold the letter along the lines that Anne creased in London. I touch my cup but the coffee has gone cold; the rain falling outside on Bay Street looks cold as well. I think the café I'm in is called *Fabulous* but I'm not sure because I've never really looked at the sign. I walk over from HMV on my lunch breaks, order a coffee, sometimes a donut, then gaze through the wall of glass at Bay Street and the Toronto Bus Terminal.

Toronto is a city that I never used to care about. Through the first three years of university here, the only thing that interested me was how to get out. The bus station became the place I would wander to when I felt homesick, knowing that at 12:40 I could hear them announce my hometown as one of the stops to be made by "Service 210 – Leaving from platform 3 in five minutes!"

I'm not homesick now. Not really. The bus station just happens to be across the street from the nicest and cheapest café within walking distance of my workplace.

Anne's letter arrived last week, and for a week now I've been daydreaming myself back to London. I pull CDs out of boxes thinking of the Monet orange sunset behind Big Ben. I walk home from school remembering the mornings I spent hackeysacking in the peace and silence of Greenwich Park. I close my eyes and see the swirl of lights and life in Leichester Square. I remember the day I left London and the morning I arrived, and more and more now, I remember a lot of broken, dissatisfying goodbyes.

PART ONE

Tennessee Williams said something akin to "memory is situated in the heart" – referring I believe to the way memories float in a goldfish bowl, bumping into one another, causing an intermingling of their separate times, characters, events. The heart retains what is special, but doesn't keep these things in a nice chronological order.

It is now mid October, and I've been back in Toronto and at U of T for a month. Since Anne's letter arrived I've been swimming in the goldfish bowl of memory. I sit in Toronto cafes drinking cold coffee and staring through windows at scattered images of the summer I spent in London. The past has risen to envelop the present, and I've become lost.

I felt the need to do something, so I bought a fresh U of T coil ring notepad and I'm filling it with memories. I'm performing an exorcism, clearing my mind of all the spirits Anne's letter has set swirling around me by trapping them on paper. At least that's the plan.

"So Peter, you do not like Mr. Phipps or Mr. Ferness?"
"Neither do you."
"I do not like Mr. Phipps," Jen said. "He is strange."
"Phipps is a walking p.h.d. for a psyche student," I began, "but at least he has a personality. Ferness is just …. I don't know… such a stuck up…."

Avi leaned forward pointing his finger at me, his face bright. "You do not like him because he always finds you doing something bad!" He looked at Jen and Anne. "When Peter started at the Benjamin he went dancing all night at a gay bar…"

"It wasn't a gay bar that night. I went with some girls I met from Winnipeg."

"Well it was Le Café de Paris, yes?"
"Wait! Avi, this isn't even the right story!"
"Right story! I didn't yet start the story!"

"The morning I got caught by Ferness wasn't after Le Café de Paris. It was the morning I didn't get any sleep because you and I passed out on the night bus and ended up in the country somewhere."

Avi leaned back and started laughing. Jen turned to me, "What country?"

I waved my hand and took a drink of beer. "That, again, is another story. I'll tell you the one Avi started. I went dancing all night at Le Café de Paris, which is in Leichester, with some girls I met from Winnipeg. We danced until 6:00a.m., took a cab back to their place near Gloucester Road, then I walked to work." I stopped and looked over at Avi. "Hey Avi, this is the right story."

"I know it is the right story. I know your stories better than you."

"Anyway, the point is I was almost late plus I hadn't had any sleep. I was the only porter that morning and when I arrived Phipps was having a heart attack because there was luggage piling up at reception so I threw my uniform on quick downstairs, grabbed some luggage and got into the lift. As I was going upstairs I undid my jacket and my pants a little so I could tuck my shirt in…"

"And your shoes were off."

"And I wanted to adjust my socks too, so the elevator stops, the doors open and Ferness is standing there and I'm balancing on one foot my pants dangling just above my knees and my jacket open."

Anne burst out laughing and Jen smiled, shaking her head. Avi looked at me with a huge grin, "And you tripped Ferness with a hoover."

"I didn't trip him with a hoover. He tripped over a hoover that I happened to be moving."

"It was in the morning," Avi leapt in, glancing from Anne to Jen. "Mr. Ferness ordered tea and muffins from the sitting room and then he came down to the kitchen to check on them. I followed him back up to the sitting room carrying the tray and when he entered the room I heard something drop and then Mr. Ferness falls forward and Peter comes out from beside the entrance with a hoover in his hand." The light chuckle turned into a laugh and he couldn't finish the story.

PART ONE

"Mulu had left the hoover sitting in the middle of the room and I didn't want her to get in trouble so I picked it up and when I was beside the door I dropped the, you know, the head of it, the long neck part, and just when I did Ferness comes waltzing in."

"And that is why you do not like Mr. Ferness – because you are always doing something when you meet him."

Anne took a drink then brushed her fingers against her lips. "You're lucky, Petey. I'm surprised they haven't fired you."

I looked at Avi. "They wouldn't fire me, would they?"

Avi drained his pint and stood up. "I do not think they would fire you. You are very good most of the time."

"Where are you going?"

He held up four fingers. "Four more pints."

The Benjamin is located just off Brompton Road where South Kensington ends and Knightsbridge begins, near the Brompton Oratory. It is a small, very expensive, 36 room hotel. It stands anonymously on a street that runs around in a circle, all the buildings connected together, all identical grey brick design, the Benjamin having only two British flags hanging over the entrance archway to set it apart.

It is owned by one upper class Brit, and managed by another, and though I had problems with both of them, the rest of the staff were wonderful. The people in management, like the head butler and head chef, were slightly older, and had to some extent settled into their careers. The rest of us, the maids, the porters, receptionists, kitchen staff, were all young and most of us were foreign – Avi was Moroccan as were about three of the maids and one of the other porters. Anne was American and Jen and I were both Canadian.

In the afternoons one of the porters had to take a drink cart around to all the rooms and restock the minibars. There was a small bar fridge in each room, usually in the closet, which was stocked with soft drinks and beer and Perrier water. You knocked on the door, if no one answered you went in with your pass key and replaced whatever the guest had used.

I interrupted an older lady napping in one of the rooms once. She was about sixty, curled up in a sofa chair napping by the window, wearing one of the hotel bath robes which were white and thick, a *Fodor's Great Britain* lying open on her lap.

She didn't answer when I knocked but I woke her up when I opened the door. I groaned lightly as I saw her raise her head from its sleeping position against the chair. "I'm sorry, I was just going to check the minibar. I can come back if you like."

"Oh no bother, go ahead." She looked out the window and yawned. "It is so beautiful outside I almost feel guilty for being in the hotel, but I became so tired shopping with my husband that I had to come back and take a nap."

I had the fridge door open, checking a few soft drinks off my list. I turned back to her. "I know how you feel, it gets tiring making your way through all the people on the streets in this heat."

"Oh," she said, "I was too tired to even finish shopping at Harrod's."

I nodded and went out to my cart for a couple bottles of Perrier water. When I returned she was dozing again, sunlight shining on her face and on the book in her lap. Through the window behind her I could see blue sky and the tops of a few of the green trees that stood in the garden behind the hotel. I tried to open the fridge door and leave without waking her but her head lifted and she caught me as I was moving towards the door. "Would you happen to know of a nice restaurant near here?"

I spun on my heel to face her again. She was smiling, sitting in the sunlight with a peaceful, sleepy glow around her. "They'd know a few at reception, or, if you don't mind, the other porter here, Avi, eats at restaurants all the time. I could send him up if you like and he could probably pick exactly the right restaurant for you, tell you how to get there and which waiter to ask for."

"Do you not eat out very often?"

PART ONE

"No, I'm still at university and my idea of a treat is bread and jam."

"Like Paddington Bear?"

I smiled. "Yes, very much like Paddington."

She tilted her head, the sleep fading from her eyes. "Pardon me for asking, but are you English?"

I shook my head. "You've noticed my accent," I grinned. "I'm from Canada, but wait until you speak to Avi, he has a Moroccan accent. Would you like me to send him up?"

"Oh yes please, I'm intrigued now. Thank you Paddington."

"Have a nice afternoon." I closed the room door behind me. I stood in the hall and looked down at my black Doc Marten's, black slacks and the long line of gold buttons running down the front of my dark red jacket. I was trying to remember some of the Paddington stories I'd read as a child – something about a racetrack, about losing something important down a trash compactor, but the facts were gone, I could only remember nuances rather than events.

I moved to the next room, knocking on the door, slipping the passkey into the lock, and I imagine she leaned back into the sunshine and the silence, memories of a little bear found at Paddington Station in her mind, the little blue coat and rain hat, and perhaps if her memories were mixing and mingling the way Williams said they do, she was also imagining a Tigger and Piglet, a 50 year old crush on Christopher Robin bringing an unconscious smile to her lips.

I lived in New Cross. When I worked the morning shift I had to be up at 5:25 a.m. I would shower and eat toast and cereal in a daze, only becoming conscious as I drank a cup of tea standing in the morning silence gazing out the kitchen window at the sky. 6:00 a.m. found me standing on the platform at the New Cross Rail Station. I'd kick pebbles, look at the grey clouds hoping it wasn't going to rain, yawn, and try to stay away from the other morning people who were yawning and kicking pebbles as well.

FESTIVAL

Around 6:10 a train from the south would pull up and stepping inside I would invariably find the seats full of people in suits. I would stand in the doorway, looking at the light columns of a football stadium disappearing behind the train. At 6:30 I was one body among hundreds walking along Villiers Street from Charing Cross to the Embankment Tube Station. 6:45 the Underground would have conveyed me from the Embankment to South Kensington, and I would be wandering along my shortcut through Thurloe Square to reach Brompton Road.

The Benjamin had a staff entrance. From the sidewalk you went down about 15 steps, buzzed at the door, the receptionist would look at you through a video camera then release the lock on the door. I would get changed into my black slacks and red jacket in the washroom adjacent to the staffroom, then go upstairs to the reception desk and begin ushering guests in and out of the hotel.

I took to starting my morning shift slightly early, because I was only able to see Sarah for about 10 minutes each morning before the day receptionist arrived to take over for her. Sarah was beautiful. She was in her late 20's with long dark brown hair that touched just below her shoulders. She liked working the night shift so when I started at 7:00am she was on her way out of the hotel.

I strolled into reception once to find Sarah dealing with a guest. I stood behind him and batted my eyelashes at her as she had him sign his credit card slip. She smiled and asked if I could take Mr. Barthes' luggage out to the cab. I took the suitcase and daybag outside and helped the driver put them into the boot. We talked for a few minutes until the hotel door opened and Mr. Barthes came down the steps. He pressed a five pound note towards me without looking and disappeared into the cab.

Sarah was standing behind the shining dark oak of the desk when I jumped up the few steps from the street back inside the hotel to the reception area. "Good morning, Peter, are you well?"

"Yes dear."

"Have you seen Anne?"

PART ONE

I grinned. "So that's why you're still here. Have you called her?"

"It just rings on."

"She must be on her way, you know Anne, she's slightly demented." I sat down in the deep plush chair which sat at the bottom right corner of the window that looked out onto the street. The grey light tumbled in as I shifted around trying unsuccessfully to get comfortable.

"Peter, Mr. Ferness is here this morning."

"He is?" I stood up quickly. Ferness was the owner. He was about 40, an ex-army man from a wealthy family who was always popping up when I least needed him."

"I thought you knew."

"I never know. I guess that's why I always get caught."

Sarah's lips parted but the phone rang and she became engaged making a reservation. I put my hands in my pockets and spun on my heel. Through the reception window you can se the Brompton Oratory and the traffic passing on Brompton Road. I turned from the window to look at the three portraits on the walls in the lobby. I ran my fingers across the spotless antique table that stood by Ferness's chair.

I turned again and moving to leave I waved at Sarah. She motioned to me and still on the phone handed me the beeper that one of the porters had to carry. I went back down to the kitchen. As I was hanging my jacket up I heard the lock on the staff entrance buzz, the door open, then saw Anne rush by the kitchen doorway towards the staffroom.

I followed her and found her frantically turning the dial on her lock. I leaned against the doorframe and I guess she caught a look in my eye because her first words were "Shut Up."

I shrugged innocently. She opened her locker, growled, squeezed by me through the door, ran down the hall to the laundry room then ran back with one of the slim fitting black dresses that the receptionists wore. She vanished into the shower room, the door closing behind her then popping open again as she emerged tugging the neckline of her dress into a neat fit over her shoulders, her street clothes in one

FESTIVAL

hand, her heart shaped gold locket bouncing on a gold chain around her neck.

She threw her clothes into her locker, closed it and turned towards me combing her fingers through her hair. "How do I look?"

"Oh my heart is just a-twitter."

She shook her head, smiling her slightly manic, devilish smile where her eyes narrow and you can faintly see her tongue pushing against the narrow space between her barred teeth. "You're a doofus," she said as she opened the door and disappeared up the stairs to the ground floor reception area.

Anne was a year older than me. She had dropped out of an art school in Chicago after arranging a British work visa. She had been in London and at the Benjamin for about six months by the time I arrived in May, and she was staying on after I left. She had straight light brown hair, blazing eyes and a demented smile which would turn innocent whenever she burst out with something obscene which would cause us to hush and turn to confirm that that we had heard her correctly, to which she would pretend innocence and say "What?" as though she hadn't said anything that couldn't be found in a Disney movie.

After work Anne and I would sometimes wander together. We'd walk up Brompton Road past Harrod's, scamper across to the Scottish Shop then wait for a break in traffic before going up the road to Hyde Park. The park was a walk under a canopy of leaves and branches across grass covered in shadows, sprinkles of sunlight lying here and there, the Serpentine off in the distance.

We would run through the subway at Hyde Park Corner and make our way around Buckingham to the Mall. The Palace, crawling with people, kids climbing around on the lions at Queen Victoria's feet. The Mall stretched out long and quiet in the sunlight, bordered by trees, capable of looking empty even when half full of people.

Early in the summer, when Anne and I were still getting to know each other, Anne had turned to me as we walked won the middle of the Mall and said "Deja-Vu."

PART ONE

I had nodded. A few weeks previous, on another Sunday when the Mall is closed to traffic, Anne, Jen, Toby the cook and I had gone rowing on the Serpentine. Afterwards I had walked Anne to Charing Cross.

"I took a picture of you with your back to the Palace."

"Yes."

Her back had been to the sun as well. I have a photograph of a shadow standing in front of a castle.

The Maple Leaf, according to *Let's Go*, is "London's Canadian pub, ay, and a good place to satisfy that late-night urge, eh, for a pint of Molson, ay, after an evening at the theatre, eh." When I read that I wondered if the language reference in their guidebook for Canada said "Speak English like a 17th century pirate."

The Maple Leaf is basically an English pub. The only Canadian aspects are the hockey games they play on a few televisions hanging from the walls and ceiling, the sports pages from Toronto newspapers pinned to a bulletin board, and a bit more Canadian rock and roll in the air than you would find anywhere else in Britain.

I remember sitting in the pub once, gazing up at a forward squeeze through two defencemen, fire a shot a the goalie but miss by a mile, but then put the rebound coming off the boards into the back of the net while Anne babbled on about something. "You know," she said, "I've heard you walking around the hotel singing to yourself."

"So?"

"Well you talk a lot about my being crazy, but that's not exactly normal is it? Plus you get undressed in elevators and trip your boss with vacuum cleaners."

"What's your favourite movie?"

"That's another annoying thing you do. You always change the subject when I'm making a point."

"Me?"

"Yes, it's horribly annoying."

FESTIVAL

I grinned at her – the grin I have which means "Yes you're absolutely right and I know I'm wrong but that doesn't mean I'm going to cooperate with you."

Anne stuck her tongue out at me and then leaned back in her chair. "Favourite movie. I don't know, maybe Barfly. What about you?"

"Either Casablanca or Slapshot."

"Slapshot! Oh my God, that's a horrible movie!"

"I know, but I have a friend at school who says lines from it all the time and he makes it seem really funny."

"You're from Toronto?"

"No, I only go to school here. I'm from a small town to the north."

"How small?"

"Two stoplights. I have to drive an hour and a half to get to a movie theatre."

"Really?"

"Yep."

"What did you do growing up in a town that small?"

"Shovelled snow. Got lost in the forest. How long are you going to stay in London?"

"A while. So that's small town life in Canada? Shovelling snow and getting lost?

"To be honest, that's what sticks out in my mind right now."

"And you're going back to university in September?"

"Yeah. I also have to find a job to pay for school. Why did you drop out of art school anyway?"

"Hey! Did I ever tell you why I started painting?"

"No."

"Awesome!" She sat up, her eyes gleaming. "I was a kid, I don't know, about Grade 3 or 4, do you find that you can remember your childhood more easily by using grades as markers or your age?"

"I don't know."

"Can I have a drink of your beer?"

"Do you want me to get you a beer?"

PART ONE

"Not yet, this is a good story. I was sitting by the window with my notebook in my lap. I used to sketch birds and things. Eventually I realized that the shadows of the leaves outside the window were falling onto the pages of my notebook, so I traced them but as the sun set the shadows moved. I was tracing them all afternoon, creating this patchwork of leaf shaped shadows on my page. Finally the sun set and I fell asleep and my mom found me with my head in my arms on the windowsill. I asked her what the date was and I made a little entry in my notebook – August 30. On August 30 I captured the sunset."

Covent Gardens. If I was going to write about Covent Gardens would I start with the prices or tourists or the sunshine or the feeling that every day there was the same, although every single person was different?

Sunshine – an ocean of bodies a blue sky of voices and music. Close your eyes on a beach and listen to the sound that life makes.

Voices, and the tinkling of glasses, patrons at outdoor cafes, offers to tie your hair, friends beckoning friends, the laughter of the crowds, the jokes and commands and requests of the performers, all the strands of noise weaving themselves into a canopy above you – stretch out your arms and surf the sounds.

Buy a sundae at the Baskin Robbins on Longacre Street and wander down past the Spitting Image puppets past the people eating and drinking at tables in front of the Rock Garden, through the Market Building past the stalls of clocks, puppets, hats, games, sweaters, jewellery, past the restaurants and fortune tellers and painters and turn and circle and stop again and sit on the cobble stones between St. Paul's Church and the Market Building and watch the performers reeling in tourists and tourist money, then watch the subplots.

Behind the pillars of St. Paul's other performers are waiting, playing cards, bouncing tennis balls, watching their colleague, waiting for him to finish, for that crowd to disperse, minutes to pass, before

FESTIVAL

the next performer goes out to do his attention grabbing ploy, to slowly but surely attract a crowd which attracts a larger crowd, to do juggling tricks, magic tricks, building to a climatic final trick and then pass the hat around, perhaps run upstairs to the patio section of the Punch and Judy pub where people gaze down at the street and watch the show for free.

And all the rest.

The music, the string quartet playing Pachelbel, the saxophone player in front of the Rock Garden who will finish a set, light a cigarette, pat his dog and then watch you for a while.

The girls passing in long flowing Victorian dresses, advertising a restaurant along the Strand. The 100 year old waiter passing with a silver tray and a bottle of champagne in one hand and a cane in the other, the bespectacled crewcut woman carrying a "Save Jesus" placard, the Americans in loud shirts and bulging pockets, the tired children and tired seniors brushing you and backing you against the wall in narrow passages. All the people who make movement difficult and lead you to search for a quiet place, a place to watch.

I went to Covent Gardens to watch. I never gave the performers money I never ordered a drink at a café and I never talked to anyone. I did however dream the past there.

In May, when I'd only been in London for a few weeks, I was floating through the Gardens humming to myself, the sunshine on my shoulders, when the crowd parted and coming down James Street as though he was walking through the parting of the Red Sea, the boy came towards me, slowly, timelessly.

I've been having this dream for almost ten years – a small boy appears, circles me and leaves. As I had turned 15, 16, 17, and recently 22, he had remained 11 or 12, a memory or messenger from another time. Perhaps in the beginning he was even real, but I've looked through memories of my life without finding him, not the boy who sat beside me in Grade 3, not a teammate from baseball or hockey teams. As far as I can tell, he has existed only in my dream.

PART ONE

He appears of his own volition, and I watch as a play unfolds. He is always in search of something, and while he never talks to me he stops other characters in the play and they bend low to him, listening, then they start pointing and offering directions. He skirts me, circles me, never approaches me.

Then the play or the vision ends. He turns hazy and fades and I am left in my own time again. In Covent Gardens the crowd began to fill in and he darted away, fading a little more with each person he passed. I was left with a memory of his eyes, the perpetual sadness, as though with one more tiny misfortune, even an undone shoelace, he would begin to cry.

The crowd filled in and I lost him. I felt the jostling and heard the voices. I looked up into the sun and rubbed my palms together, glanced down at my feet, and moved on.

When I found my job at the Benjamin I was still living in cheap hotels, moving every couple of days, backpack on my shoulders, to even cheaper ones. I met Toby on my second day at the Benji and he introduced me to a lady he knew who had just had her youngest daughter move out of the house.

The daughter who had left was 24, two years older than me, and her mother found that she didn't like the new silence which had settled on the house, the lonely feeling of bolting the front door, turning out all the lights and lying down in bed to listen for faults in the silence. She gave me a place to live and I made her life a little noisier, pushing the silence back into the corners.

It was a great arrangement for me. I paid Tracy 65 pounds a week which included cooked meals, rent, television, phone, washing machine and a small garden. She didn't mother me but she looked after me. I left her notes when I would be out late and wouldn't be home for dinner. When we did have dinner together we would sit at the small kitchen table and watch the evening news. There was a story once about a ten year old girl who was 10p short of her bus

FESTIVAL

fare so the driver wouldn't allow her on board. She was abducted and killed as she walked home. Tracy looked at me and said "I'm getting to hate this London" and I nodded, pausing to watch the television respectfully, the way you pause before raising your head after saying "Amen."

TORONTO

I've turned out all the lights in our apartment. I feel secure now, the way a thief must feel safe and secure when dressed in darkness. I'm sitting in our living room on our broad windowsill, looking through the window at College and Bathurst. A streetcar rumbles by, heading for Spadina, silent faces gaze out the windows, tired faces.

In front of Sneaky Dee's, the bar across the street, the rhythm of Friday night street life begins. A hot dog vendor opens his Shopsy's patio umbrella, cyclists lock their bikes in front of the bank, punks, alcoholics and homeless people circle and circulate in waves of motion, heads turn, friends are recognized, feet are tapped, watches checked streets crossed, and me myself? I'm watching, waiting.

I move from the window to the couch, close my eyes and hide behind a second veil of darkness. We're having a party tonight. I returned from work an hour ago to an empty apartment. It is now 8:00, I'm the only one home, and the part of my mind which is curious is wondering if Tyler and Steve, my two roommates, are at a gas station somewhere, refilling the propane tank for Tyler's BBQ.

Generally though, I'm not curious. The bottle of wine in my hand, which I haven't mentioned yet, is half empty. I'm not worried about where people are, just vaguely interested in what they're going to do.

A Fairy Tale: Once upon a time, in two separate college residences, there lived boys and girls who were friends, who weren't

PART ONE

sleeping together, who weren't jealous of each other, and amongst whom Peter felt happy.

Peter blinked, a new school year began, and now knives are drawn. Former friends have slept together, temporary lovers have become jealous of each other, and for all Peter knows his roommates are absent because they, like Peter, are expecting fireworks tonight. Consequently they are downstairs at Bistro 222 downing large quantities of cheap, recycled beer, hoping inebriation will provide them with the emotional equivalent of a full metal jacket.

This is also the reason Peter has finished half a bottle of wine by himself in the darkness – he doesn't want to be sober tonight. He doesn't want to be drawn into discussions and arguments and emotions tonight.

I'm on the couch enveloped in darkness when I sense movement. I open my eyes but still darkness. Hands touch my shoulders, soft lips graze my cheek just after long scented hair touches my right forearm.

A voice, a whisper – "this is very depressing" and the words gently brush my ear the way a smile across a crowded room gently brightens your eyes.

A flash of light now and I close my eyes as a second, more distant voice calls out from the kitchen behind me "Pete, where are Tyler and Steve?"

Rustling in the kitchen, fridge door – bottles – fridge door. A hand slowly brushes through my hair, fingers trace the back of my neck then lift away. Buttons are pressed, the stereo hums and the fingers which parted my darkness have brought music to life.

Three hours later I've found my jacket and I'm out the door, my drunken mind even remembers to check my pocket for my keys. Everything went as I expected – my friends began to arrive, Tyler and Steve appeared, I did my Blues Brothers dance, serious conversations began in dark corners, and from dark corners sad faces requiring sympathy moved towards Peter, and, refusing to get involved, Peter ran away.

FESTIVAL

I'm running away.

I've been doing this for three years now and my journey through the dark Toronto streets is mechanical. I pass sleepwalking pedestrians barely noticing their existence, I step into pools of wet light and leave wet footsteps glowing behind me in the darkness.

University Avenue because it's deserted, the bus station, Bay Street, Front Street, Union Station, the underpass, march along, look up and you can see the CN Tower, stare straight ahead and you can see water.

I don't know why I began running here.

At the lake my pace slows, my hands cold I hide them in the cuffs and sleeves of my coat. If you know the area, and I do, you can avoid the lights and sit at the water's edge in nearly complete darkness.

And this is all I do. I listen to the waves lap against the wall, I follow the path of pilot lights on boats out on the lake, I look for signs of life out on the island.

I lean back on my bench on the deserted lakeshore and I watch the stars. Borealis, the north star of my era but not the north star of the Pharaohs and not the north star which will guide future generations. I conjure up an image of Kepler and place him on the lakeshore with me, his arms outstretched his face to the starlight. When he deciphered the movements of the planets he wrote "I am free to give myself up to the sacred madness." He had unravelled one of the mysteries of life, he had taken a step closer to his God, and I like to think of him staring at the sky, his heart glowing with the beauty of the world.

I sit on the shore of Lake Ontario watching the night sky with Kepler, glad that he is listening to the celestial music of the spheres, but when the wind brushes my ear it is to carry the sound of the stars whispering themselves into ashes, whispering themselves into dust.

PART ONE

A postcard from Alberta, from my sister. My brother who lived in Hamilton but installed electrical gizmos throughout southern Ontario didn't write to me at all while I was away, but he and the written word didn't get along and I wasn't surprised. He would be far more likely to show up in person, brushing away my amazement with a question about the location of the nearest pub.

My sister however had had a shelf on which she put books she wanted me to read. She had completed a Masters program, words were simple tools to her, but until I wrote to her only a postcard came my way – the Alberta Badlands.

I read it in Tracy's garden on one of my days off. I was reading a book and when I went inside to make another cup of tea I found that the mail had arrived. The baby was doing such and such now, her husband Bill had hurt his foot and been home with her for a few days, she hoped I was enjoying myself. This wasn't the Hannah I remembered. It was a postcard from someone's wife, someone's mother, not my sister, not the Hannah who held my hand in hers when we went to the CNE, my brother pestering my parents ahead of us, but Hannah with me, making sure I was okay. I thought of the dumb doll games she used to make me play with her and her friends, of being embarrassed to death in public school when she'd chase after me, a Grade 7 chasing after a Grade 2, and kiss me in the schoolyard.

Then there was her look. I usually resisted Hannah's entreaties to play games with her. She'd say "please Peter play" for a while, then she'd stop cajoling me and look hurt, staring at me with teary eyes, and to prevent her from crying I'd break down and say "okay okay" and she'd brighten and put a bonnet on my head and a teddy bear in my arms and invariably my brother would return from some baseball game with a bunch of sweating thug friends.

I put the Alberta Badlands card down and found my page in the book I was reading, wishing vaguely that the Hannah I remembered would write me a letter.

23

FESTIVAL

"What'd you do that for?"

Anne kicked at a stone then bent to pick it up. "I'm going to do it again." She narrowed her eyes like a baseball pitcher both accepting the catcher's sign and focusing on his location, then threw the rock at the window she had missed the first time. She hit the glass but the glass didn't break. She swore and started searching for another rock and I looked up at the sun and ran my hand through my sunwarmed hair.

When you cross Tower Bridge to the south side of the Thames, and move east, time seems to have stopped. The buildings are dead relics from Dickens' generation – low faded brown brick ghosts tumbling in on themselves. The streets are narrow and twisting and deserted even at high noon.

Anne and I were wandering. I had been trying to keep the river in view on my right but the street had met a wall and turned left, and now we hadn't seen the river, a shop, a pub, or another person, for about fifteen minutes, and Anne was pelting the windows of a hapless old building with rocks.

I knelt in the shadow cast by the building opposite the one Anne had turned her attention on. Anne threw, missed, swore, and I, with my arm full of fifteen years of baseball, knelt to the side of the action, watching Anne's loose brown hair dance when she threw.

To my right, the direction from which we had come, the street disappeared in a sharp right turn around a stranded green knoll, a small oasis amid these dusty streets and buildings. To my left, around 100 metres away, the street hit a wall, splitting left and right in a T shape.

I put my fingers over my eyes and in this imperfect darkness listened to the soft /t/'s and /k/'s of Anne's stones, Anne's muttered curses, her footsteps on the street, and slowly, in the heat of the day, I drifted away.

I liked this part of town and periodically I would walk into London from New Cross, going up past Surrey Quays and Rotherhithe until I hit the river, then just heading west until I came to Tower Bridge. I'd found that I knew these narrow grimy streets even before I saw them. They were the streets that Defoe had described in *Journal of the Plague Year*, the streets that ran like veins through Dickens' novels.

I found however that they didn't have much life other than that attributed to them in the books I had read. Covent Gardens had life, Hyde Park, Brompton Road, the tourist areas, but the streets of southeast London would have meant nothing to me if I hadn't been able to fill them with the past – watch the Great Fire leap from building to building, the police barricade suspected carriers of the Plague into their own houses, leaving families to rot together. I found the present dead so I used literature to help me recreate the past, meanwhile Anne was hurling stones at windows.

The sound of breaking glass pushed back the silence of the deserted street. I opened my eyes and saw Anne flash a grin and flick me a stone. "Your turn," she said, as though we had agreed to take turns breaking all the glass on this street. Break all the windows break all the glass, reach out instead of look out, but I had spent my life sympathizing with the glassmaker – respecting the care and labour and patience behind each pane of glass, the protection glass affords against chaos, the loneliness behind glass walls.

I stood up and dropped the stone back into Anne's hand and in one movement she turned, raised her arm and fired the stone through another window, the street echoing with the sound of falling glass.

She turned and smiled at me, the smile one sibling gives another which means "I've found out where mom hides our Christmas presents, but I'm not going to tell you." We stepped side by side through the sunlight, heading towards the T in the street where we would have to decide between left and right, figure out how we were going to get into town.

"I'm lost by the way Anne."

She shrugged, looking up at the sun, her right hand toying with her gold heart shaped locket. "It's alright. I know the magic word."

"What's the magic word?"

"You moron," she laughed, "don't you know?"

I shrugged.

FESTIVAL

"Everyone knows the magic word," her eyes gleaming, grinning at me, "it starts with an A."

Your route to the Swan and Garter depends on what zones your travelcard is good for. In London Zone 1 is where everybody wants to go, and Zone 2 is where everybody wants to live, so most travelcards are valid for 1 and 2, but the Swan and Garter pub in Putney is narrowly within Zone 3.

Anne, Sarah, Jen, Avi and I all had Zone 1 and 2 cards. We got off the District Line at Putney Bridge, crossed the river and walked the rest of the way to the pub. That was 8:00pm, early evening.

The Swan is beautiful. The high ceiling and long straight main room remind you of a tall Amish barn. The wall which faces the river is composed mainly of glass and as we sat telling stories and drinking, I would often steal away from the others, lean back in my chair and retreat from the conversation, gazing through the windows at the river.

The Thames in Putney, as in Greenwich, looks like a real river. When you stand on Westminster Bridge and gaze east you see derelict hulks anchored in the river, bleeding rust into the water. In Putney trees bend close to the river, two man sculls flash by, and if you dropped a line into the water and tried your hand at fishing you might actually believe that whatever you caught would be safe to eat.

I returned from one of these reveries once to see that I had a new pint in my hand and that Avi was telling a joke to Jen in French, which she was translating into English for Sarah, Anne and me. The punch line came and not having heard most of the joke I didn't get it. I laughed though, I pretended I had been listening, that I was participating. I watched Jen blush slightly, Avi in a T Shirt and cream coloured vest raise his glass to his lips, Anne wind into one of her semi-obscene stories and Sarah, with her long dark brown hair, gentle features and perfect lines cause heads to turn, men passing to wish that they were sitting where I was.

PART ONE

Just after 11:00 we were crossing the river again, heading for home. I lagged behind, touching a hand on the rail of the bridge, looking down at the still, night-bound water. I watched the river flow into darkness, scanned the shorelines for secrets, and was only brought away from my transfixiation with nothing by hearing my name called.

I turned and saw the others swirling ahead of me, laughing, Anne and Avi and Jen and Sarah almost glowing in the night. They left the bridge and stepped onto land and I stumbled after them, tripping through the darkness.

"Where did you go last night?"

Avi smiled and tipping his tiny china cup finished his coffee. "Peter, Peter," he said, shaking his head, smiling. "Coffee or tea?"

"Coffee please, in a real cup."

He poured coffee into one of the staff mugs then refilled his cup, one of the beautiful china ones that the guests used. I took my cup from him and putting a hand on my shoulder he led me out of the kitchen to the staff canteen.

"What time did you leave last night?" he asked.

"I don't know, after you. We looked for you but you were gone."

"Hello Mulu! How are you?"

Mulu smiled. "Late!" Avi held the door open for her and she brushed between us into the hall. Avi called something to her in Arabic which prompted an embarrassed "AVI!" to ring in the hall.

I sat down at the staffroom table and Avi went to open the window which only looked onto the staff staircase but still allowed light in, and on a morning like this, the smell of the rain which was falling upon the city.

"I don't know where I met her," he began. I smiled, it was to be one of Avi's stories about women. He found them and lost them the way other people lose matches or pens. "What do you call when you can't remember something?"

27

"Bad memory?"

"No. When you are fine, you know where you are and what you are doing, then an hour later you are somewhere else and you don't remember what happened."

"Blackouts. You had a blackout."

Two fingers appeared. Avi liked to illustrate his conversations with his hands. "I had two blackouts." He sipped some coffee and searched his pockets for his cigarettes. "I opened my eyes last night and I was in a McDonald's. I do not know where, and across the table a girl was eating chips. She was beautiful but I did not know her."

"What'd she look like?"

"Brown hair, to here," he touched his shoulder. "White shirt with a vest, very nice breasts, very nice eyes."

"You met her at Crown Royale, you were talking with her at our table."

"So I had a blackout and woke up at McDonald's. She was talking to me about her job and then I said *Who are you?* And she laughed. *Oh my God!* she said, *we don't even know each other's names! I'm Alice.* I said my name and then I had another blackout.

"And you woke up in her arms in a little wooden cottage in Surrey."

He shook his head, grinning as he tapped the ashes from his cigarette. The staffroom door opened and Jen came in, wearing street clothes, a backpack hanging from one shoulder, her hair wet. "Jennifer!" Avi shouted. "Bonjour, comment vas-tu?"

She waggled her head with her "okay" smile. "Il fait froid cette matin, non?"

"Compared to London or Canada?"

"Compared to Morocco it is cold."

"You are both on duty now?" Jen asked. Avi and I both nodded and Jen shook her head. "So very very easy to be a porter. Sit drinking coffee all morning."

She shrugged her backpack down her arm and hung her jacket on the coat rack. I nodded at Avi. "So if you didn't wake up in Surrey, where did you wake up?"

PART ONE

"Ah," he tapped his cigarette. "In a kitchen. It was very late now. I was sitting eating cereal at a table." He paused and grinned, shaking his head. "It was very strange," he said. "I stood up and found my jacket, and when I went into the hall I hear a shower running but I didn't want to stay so I went down some stairs and found the door and went outside and guess where I was?"

He looked at me positively beaming. I looked at Jen who had sat down across from me and had her elbow on the table and her hand supporting her chin. "Je n'sais pas Avi."

"Finsbury Park! Two down from my building!" He had his two fingers in the air, his eyes beaming, he was absolutely delighted. "I was putting my jacket on outside the house, thinking I would have to find an underground sign then I thought *I have been here before*, then I went into the street and looked at my building and I thought *that is my building.*"

Avi started chuckling and Jen looked at me questioningly. "Avi met a girl last night but he was drinking flaming zambuckis and he started having blackouts."

"Ah. Avi you will have to take some cereal to her house, knock on the door and say *Can I make breakfast for you? I have brought the cereal.*"

I drained my coffee and stood up. It was time for me to put in an appearance at reception. "And wine. Cereal and wine."

I opened the staffroom door and waved at Jen as I stepped into the hall. Avi said "she will think I am crazy" as the door closed behind me."

I took off my red jacket and hung it up on the rack. The porters only had to wear the jackets when we were around the guests. They were too hot to wear when working in the kitchen preparing breakfast trays or tea services. The kitchen was practically split into two smallish rooms by a large unit that sat in the middle of the room. On our side, near the entrance to the kitchen, the unit was a high cupboard with

FESTIVAL

spaces to store cups and coffeepots and trays, and enough room to set several trays side by side as we were preparing meals.

On the other side, the cook's side, were the stoves and oven and microwave which backed against the cupboard. There was a little storeroom for food on that side of the kitchen and a large freezer as well. The kitchen was on the garden side of the building and there were two windows on the garden wall, the tops of which reached ground level, allowing sunlight to shine in.

Toby was on the cooking side of the kitchen, unhurriedly preparing the staff lunch. Toby was about 25, a cockney with short straw coloured hair, pale skin, and slightly yellow fingertips from his years of smoking. He was the head chef, which made him part of management, but I rarely thought of him as being a manager. One night when we were on the late shift I pestered him until he resorted to soaking me with the kitchen dishwashing hose. It's hard to think of someone who does that as your boss.

I filled a glass with milk and nodded at Toby. "What's for lunch?"

"Chicken and vegetables. Good for you."

"Not for me. I'm allergic to vegetables."

"Yeah?" he was bent over, peering into the oven.

"Yep. Vegetables and meat loaf. I swell up like a big swelled up thing."

Toby shook his head as he pulled the pan of chicken breasts and legs and wings out of the oven. "Pity," he answered.

I heard voices behind me. Ruth and Jen had come in to get their lunch, both with drops of perspiration on their foreheads. Ruth was fanning herself with the white apron that the maids wore over their pink dress. Ruth was in her mid 20's, from Kenya with very dark black skin which made her smile seem brilliant. She was a few inches shorter than my 5'8, and she was very thin.

"Peter," she said, "what time you start?"

"7:00."

"I did not see you this morning."

"I've been in the garden playing football with Ferness."

PART ONE

"Oh yes, this boy," she said, trying to get by me to the food, "very very bad."

My favourite thing about wandering the hotel checking the minibars in the afternoons was the opportunity it provided to bother the maids. I would pull my drink cart out of the lift and see the maid's trolley of towels and bedsheets parked against the wall. I would look down the hall to see which room door was open, sneak in and try to startle the maid. I remember peeking my head into a room and seeing Ruth ripping the sheets off the bed. I waited until she had her back to me, putting new pillowcases on the pillows, then I snuck up behind her and whispered "boo" in her ear.

She lurched forward onto the bed, then turned to me her eyes wide. "Peter! It must have been, I knew it was you."

I smiled and walked to the closet to check the minibar. "How are you Ruth, busy?"

"No. I am here until 5:00 today," she held up two fingers, "and I have only two rooms left to do. I am going very slow."

I checked a few drinks off on my list and went out to my cart to get replacements. "Well, if you don't have anything to do why don't we go find Jen or Mulu and jump on their beds."

"So bad this boy!" she laughed, shaking her head. "When are you going home to your girlfriend?" This had been a joke that Ruth had played with all summer. Since Avi and I went drinking so often, and since I usually told Ruth my stories about meeting girls and dancing with them at clubs like the Hippodrome, she had assumed I was some sort of ladies-man. She also assumed that I had a girlfriend at home who I was cheating on."

"I promise you Ruth, there are no girls crying about me to their mothers in Canada."

"This boy – you never tell the truth."

I closed the fridge and moved towards the door. "Well, at least my nose hasn't started growing yet. See you later Ruth."

Ruth was kind of like Jen. They both had happy souls and they were fun to be around. Ruth actually had a degree in hotel management or something from a university in Kenya. I didn't think it was any of my business so I didn't ask why she was working as a maid in London. If she had left Kenya because she could make more money in England I felt sorry for her. I wasn't making any money and I wasn't even being taxed. Ruth and the others were making just slightly more than they needed to pay their bills each week, and unlike Jen and Anne and I, this wasn't just a summer job for them, this was their life.

I was buzzing around a room once when Ruth walked in, an awed look on her face. She waved at me to follow her and led me down to a room on her floor. She pointed at a chair which had been moved from its usual spot and placed beside the bed. An ashtray was sitting on a fifty pound note on the chair.

She shook her head slowly. "Is it true?"

Ruth hadn't cleaned the room yet. The bed was a mess with sheets on the floor, pillows everywhere, a garbage can on its side, the contents spilling onto the floor. This room had had the same occupants for about a week – Italians whose luggage I had brought in. Judging by how much time they had spent in their room, they were probably also newlyweds. I put a hand on Ruth's shoulder, "They moved the chair and put the ashtray on top. They didn't forget it."

She shook her head, still trying to absorb the idea of finding that much money as a tip. "I did not believe it, so I went for you." She stepped towards the chair and picked the note up, the amazement on her face being replaced by a gradually brightening smile. "Peter!"

I put my arm around her shoulder and she turned that into a hug, her face bright now as though she was giving the sunshine back to the sky. "I have to show Mulu!" she shouted, running out of the room.

PART ONE

TORONTO

Toronto mornings 6:45a.m. – turn off an alarm and turn on your body.

Shower entices your reluctant soul to come home, the newspaper twinges your mind, steam rises from your tea in a ballet of constant motion, and slowly, slowly, rises the courage of the early morning.

8:15a.m. feet touch sidewalk, hands slide into gloves, head back blow your frosty breath into the late autumn air.

The College street landmarks slide by – the firestation and clocktower, Massimo's Pizza, the Spadina intersection where Chinatown begins. After two and a half months I march along without noticing anymore, skating, sliding, Toronto sails by like the hydro poles I watch through the window when the bus carries me home.

HMV – His Majesty's Voice. As soon as it opened it became THE music store in Toronto. I don't know why. I don't know why I stay. I hate the building, the roaring music, 99% of the customers, and I don't even particularly like the people I work with.

So my mind shuts down. Under their own power my hands open boxes, remove CDs, put CDs on shelves. My voice says things like "Jazz and and Classical are upstairs" all on its own.

This is my day in and day out (*Work all day, what do you get? Another day older and deeper in debt.*)

And on Wednesdays and Thursdays?

Punch clock at 6:00pm run out onto Yonge Street along Edward past the World's Biggest Bookstore and head north towards campus. Wednesday is *Russian History*, Thursday is *Quebec Politics*. I sit in class daydreaming, wondering why I'm there, the professor's comments about Kruschev or Rene Levesque the furthest things from my mind.

A friend of mine from highschool got in touch with me last month and made me take the bus to Waterloo to meet her and another friend of ours who is at Laurier University. The friend who called me has a real job already. She did a quick ECE degree and now she teaches Kindergarten.

It had been three years and the conversation was slow and stilted until later when we were drunk. I told London stories, my Laurier friend bemoaned women, and the teacher talked about cutbacks, class sizes, and hell spawned children, things that only other teachers could truly understand and which she could only laugh about when drunk.

I was surprised at how quickly it all came back – the inside jokes, the easy laughter and sympathy of people with a shared history, the power of our common experiences to overcome the awkwardness of three years of separation.

I crashed on the floor of my Laurier friend's apartment, since he had sold his couch in order to buy groceries. Hung over I took the bus back to Toronto the next day. Travelling on the 401, more interested in the view through the window than the book in my hand, I found myself questioning why I had made that trip.

After three years I had spent an evening with people from another time, people I might not see for another three years. Was I going to start trying to tie together all the different parts of my life? Wouldn't it just be easier to keep letting things slide away?

Anne wouldn't have wasted a second on this question, but she and I are very different. When Anne looks back on her life she'll see Chicago and London and everything else as a series of interconnected chapters which will have built a single book. But my life is a series of clean breaks. My life is a series of books which I finish at a bus station, drop on a bench, travel storyless to a new city, where I buy another $10.00 paperback, lick my finger turn the first page and begin an entirely new story, an entirely new life, and when people ask about the past I have to pause and look away, turning back the pages in my mind, and sometimes the answers don't come. Sometimes I've forgotten too perfectly.

Wednesday and Thursday nights I leave the Sydney Smith building the back way, travel along College Street in the 9:00pm darkness, turn my key in the first lock, trip up the stairs, turn another

PART ONE

key, throw some frozen fishsticks in the oven and at 11:00 I collapse on my battered mattress on the hardwood floor.

Count sheep, count past lives, past Peters.

Drift, doze, dream, daylight.

6:30a.m. and what do you get?

∽

The only decoration I had in my room at Tracy's was an Ontario road map which I had pinned to the wall. I didn't feel I was going to be around long enough to put my stamp on the room, plus I didn't want to ruin Tracy's walls.

The room was very small. The window looked out at the quiet street, as did Tracy's, her room being beside mine. I had a small closet, a wicker chair, a dresser, bedside table with a lamp and a single bed. That left me just enough room on the floor to do sit ups.

I never went to Avi's apartment in Finsbury but I did go to Anne's place. She had posters and plants, her room smelled of the perfume she wore, her room reminded you of her.

Tracy's house likewise was Tracy's house. Pictures of her children and grandchildren hung on the walls, amongst the videos were titles like *Family Christmas 1995*, the phone rang and I would take messages from one daughter to be given to Tracy to pass on to another daughter.

But there used to be more. There used to be comings and goings and footsteps on the stairs and people to talk to at mealtimes. The house was no longer full of voices, it was full of echoes, and Tracy needed a boarder the way sailors need a buoy in the ocean, to show how far they were drifting, how far the waves had pushed them from land. Tracy needed a boarder as a signpost, something to point her away from memories towards shore, towards real life, and the funny thing is that I may have been able to do that for her, just by being there, just by making her want to take a little more care over dinner than she used to, just by leaving my periodic notes telling her what I was doing.

FESTIVAL

Anne was asleep. She seemed peaceful, at ease, and she was I guess, that was the kind of person she was, at ease with herself, happy within herself. Eckhart's theory applied to Anne – *Do not seek for God outside your own soul*, and Anne didn't.

We were returning to London from Dover. I'd wanted to see the white cliffs and I'd also had a dream about drinking wine on a grassy bluff looking out over the English Channel, waiting for the Armada, and Anne had gone with me. I don't know how long I watched her, but it was early evening and shadows were stretching across the fields when she awoke.

"The ticket guy was here while you were sleeping. This is a first class car and our tickets are only coach tickets."

"Do we have to move?"

"He was nice. It's a slow night, there's hardly anybody on the train, he just said to be careful next time."

"How long have I been asleep?"

I looked at my watch. "Under an hour."

"What have you been doing?"

"Well besides being a motor-mouth when you're awake, you also talk when you're asleep, and I guess I've been getting to know the real you."

Anne snorted. "What's the real me like?"

"I don't want to scare you."

"Oh bull." She sat up in the long seat across from me, shaking her head, running her hands through her long brown hair, then she stood up facing the window, stretching her hands towards the ceiling of the compartment. She opened the window and stood gazing outside, watching the fields roll by, shadows creep across the land.

After a few minutes she sat down in her seat, still looking out the window. "This is nice huh? Travelling by train."

I shrugged.

"Trains are much better than planes."

I shrugged again.

PART ONE

"With trains you get a feeling for the journey, the distance between your beginning and your destination. With planes you just sit in this big room with a bunch of screaming kids and old women who spill coffee on your jeans, you watch a movie eat food and then you're in another country and you have no appreciation for the journey you've taken, you've no real idea how you got from point A to point B."

I looked at her and found her looking at me, which made me slightly uncomfortable. I turned to the window, the countryside, and guessed that I was more or less facing west, facing home.

"Do you have any brothers or sisters Anne?"
"I have a younger brother. Radek. He's two years younger than me. I always had to look after him at recess when we were in public school."

"You were the little tomboy bodyguard?"

"Yep, I was little Annie Oakley. What about your family?"
"I'm the youngest. I have a brother four years older and a sister five years older. She's married now, she has a baby girl."

Anne leaned her head back against the seat, her eyes narrowed. We had walked a lot that day, plus we'd finished the bottle of wine I had carried in my knapsack. Anne actually looked like she was going to fall asleep again. "What was it like growing up with your brother and sister so much older?"

"I don't know. Natural. I don't have anything to compare it with."

"Still…"

She was nudging words out of me, a tactic that I usually resisted with people. I like half-truths and convoluted stories, I like shades of mystery to protect me like smoke screens – *Pay no attention to the man behind the curtain*. I feel better when people are unsure what to think about me. But Anne was another jester, and by the time I left England we had a profound knowledge of the other's riddles. I would look behind her wall of laughter to see darker thoughts, and she would invert my stories to find the way back to the truth.

I ran my hand through my hair and touched my fingers to the glass of the window. "I'm the only one who doesn't remember the first house my parents had, where my brother and sister lived for about ten years." The pale blue sky was beginning to turn grey outside. Anne responded with silence and the silence prodded me on. "We have four or five photo albums at home. The last two include me, the house I remember, my dog, our car, the way my parents look is the way I remember them. Then there are the earlier ones, the early years of my brother and sister. There is a different house, different friends, and my parents look different, younger, with a sense of joy in their faces, the joy of this being their first encounter with parenthood.

"I remember looking through those albums once on my own. I was a kid and it felt like the first time I'd seen those pictures, but it probably wasn't. I sat there in one of those timeless states when a child is absorbed in something, looking through photos of my brother and sister's birthday parties, young looking aunts and uncles holding them aloft, and I wondered *When did this happen?* and felt jealous because I wasn't there. It was as though my brother and sister had lived in a totally different world, one that I had been excluded from. I had a happy childhood, idyllic even, but I grew up wondering if the things I was experiencing were real, if there was a secret history which I was unaware of, if photos would surface to reveal another world I had missed and devalue the one I was living in."

It was a beautiful summer night, it seemed like we were alone on a privately hired train, heading back to London after a day of exploring. The sleep had left Anne's face and she was staring at me. I met her eyes.

"I used to act in highschool," she said, her voice soft. She turned from me to the window, the fields rolling by, then finally to her hands in her lap. "I would be on stage, sitting on a chair at a table, the wall behind me looking like a room in a house, then the curtains would close and the stagehands would rush out to change the scene while we changed our costumes. The curtain would open and I'd be standing in a field, at a bus stop, on the deck of a boat. I began to think that in life there were little elves and gremlins who changed the scenes. You walk down a street which has been arranged for you, the movements of other people choreographed around you, you step into a store and frantically they make the sun set a little lower, shift

PART ONE

a cloud, add new people and subtract others, then when you step outside again everything is ready.

"Night is the big scene change. They mess up your hair, add wrinkles around your eyes, slip a newspaper under your door, and the next morning is a brand new scene."

"And someday, if you turn fast enough, maybe you'll see an elf scurrying around a corner."

"Yeah."

Anne and I both looked outside. I touched my fingers to the window as the train rolled through England.

TORONTO

I want to say that I'm never at home, but *Never* is a big word, and *Home* is an ambiguous one. There are days when I neither have to work or go to school, and on those days most of my time is spent at the apartment.

My days off always feel like Sundays, although they hardly ever are. I wake early, walk up Lippincott Street to the laundromat and spend an hour and a half there, reading Neruda or something until my clothes are done. I go home, grab my school backpack and start weaving north to the grocery store on Bloor just west of Spadina.

That's the morning.

I spend lunch eating pea soup in our living room, amused by the sight, unfamiliar for me, of midday sunlight shining through our window. Steve and Tyler awake separately on the floor above me. I hear one shower start and finish, footsteps, mutters, then another shower, then Tyler's girlfriend calls and he's busy on the phone in his room for an hour.

Steve comes down, makes toast and cereal, sits with me in the living room talking about school or girls, then he's off to some quasi-girlfriend's place to spend the day creating more trouble for himself.

FESTIVAL

I go up to my room, look out the window for a few minutes, then sit down at my desk and thumb through the notes I've been making for my latest essay. The day passes, dinner is prepared and eaten, around 9:00 we call a friend or two and head up to Rower's for wings and beer.

And that, maybe once every two weeks since we've lived here, is the time I spend at home.

The rest of my time is spent on the streets, my feet shuffling through leaves and rain and snow - east on College in the morning, west at night, always coming and going, never being anywhere.

As recently as this summer I would have said that I felt more at ease, more at *Home*, in this state of perpetual motion than I did at rest, but that's not true anymore. When I walk home in the evening the sight of my two solitary feet pounding the sidewalk fills me with regret rather than security.

I used to believe that on the streets, in motion, there were no lies, no expectations of permanence, while at rest you live in a permanent state of denial – you try to flush out the edges of a life, believing that what you're creating will last, will resist change, only to have the seasons turn, telephone numbers disconnected, rituals abandoned.

I used to feel at ease within the nothingness of motion, justifying this ease by saying that change could never hurt me if I believed in nothing but change. But the streets are very cold when you believe that they don't lead anywhere, and I have been cold for a very long time, spending the best part of myself within change, within nothing, refusing life the ability to hurt me by refusing to have a life.

❦

"I guess this would be a bad time for me to steal some breakfast?"

Avi grinned and gave me a "Yes this is a bad time" nod. He and Katya and Lisa, the two breakfast waitresses who only worked until 11:30, were bustling around the kitchen as though every guest in the hotel had just ordered breakfast.

PART ONE

Avi started filling a teapot with boiling water and looked at me over his shoulder. "Peter, go to reception and see if there is luggage and come back in ten minutes."

I took my red porter's jacket off the rack. As I walked up the stairs to the lobby I did up the buttons, the tight one at the neck which I hated I did last. Sarah was at the reception desk smiling at some guests who were checking out, her long dark brown hair tied back.

Sarah nodded upon seeing me, a faint smile coming to her lips. "Peter, can you take Mr. and Mrs. Franklin's luggage out to the cab please?"

I picked up two of their suitcases and glanced at Mrs. Franklin. I had checked them in a few days ago and when I had finished moving their luggage she had come out into the hall with me holding a ten pound bill in her hand and said "Where shall I put this?"

I took their first two cases outside and went back in for the third one. Mrs. Franklin followed me outside this time, her husband staying at the desk to sign bills with Sarah. They weren't rich but they were in the highest levels of middle class, like most of the guests who came to the Benjamin. She had shoulder length red hair, rings all over her fingers and she was wearing a dress suit. When I put the suitcase down she stood in front of me, holding out another ten pound note. She smiled, and maybe it was just me, but her tongue seemed to be abnormally visible. "Here you go darling, thank you very much."

We were standing in front of the hotel, the taxi beside us, the sky grey above us. It was a cool morning, the breeze ruffled the note in her hand as I reached for it, watching her watching me. I stood there for a few seconds wondering what she was doing – coming from a small town you hear about flirtatious women but never really believe that they exist.

I smiled. "What's going on?"

She looked down at my feet and slowly lifted her eyes up to my face again. "You aren't English are you?"

"No, and you must be American."

"Yes. I knew you weren't English because you have more colour in your face than the English do."

"Yes, well, thank you. Goodbye maam."

I moved slightly towards the steps but she stood still. "Is that all?"

I turned on my bashful look, muttered "I'm sorry" and moving to the car opened the door. She stepped towards me, into the V formed by the car and the open door, and offered me her hand. "Wouldn't you at least like to shake my hand?"

I reached over the car door and slowly, and awkwardly, shook her hand. The hotel door opened and Mr. Franklin walked out onto the top of the steps. I dropped his wife's hand, scooted up the steps past Mr. Franklin without looking at him and entered the reception which was empty now save for Sarah standing alone behind the desk. "Hey," I said, "you know what that freakshow woman was doing?"

"Peter!"

"She was flirting with me with her husband just inside here."

Sarah's eyes widened and she nodded towards the doorway to the small computer room behind the desk.

"What?"

Phipps came out of the computer room and around the desk with a folder in his hands. He nodded silently, looking me up and down. I started to worry that I hadn't done up one of the buttons on my uniform. "Tim, did you shave this morning?"

I touched my fingers to my cheek, ignoring the fact that he had forgotten my name again. They used to have a porter at the hotel who looked somewhat like me, but who had left well before I arrived. His name had been Tim, and Phipps had been unable to keep the two of us separate.

"Where do you live?" he asked, before I had time to answer his first question.

"New Cross."

"Hm mmm." He nodded at me, turning God knows what over in his mind. "That is a considerable drive early in the morning."

"I take the train Mr. Phipps."

PART ONE

"Yes, well then let's not do it again right?"
"Sir?"
He waved his hand in the general direction of my face. "Well your appearance, Tim. We can't have the staff looking like brutes now can we? We have to consider the guests." He moved past me towards the hall. He looked like an outcast weasel, scurrying around in his blue suit trying to do something good to be readmitted to the family.

I looked at Sarah who shrugged and smiled. "Don't worry, you're looking cute as always."

"He said I look like a brute."
"He's quite a one."
"One what?"
"A one."
"What does that mean?"
"He's quite a character."
"Oh. Is that my British English lesson for the morning?"
"Yes Peter."
"At home we'd call him a *knob*."

Sarah stood up slightly on tiptoes and pointed behind me. "You'd probably best leave now. Mr. Ferness just stepped out of a cab."

I looked over my shoulder out the window then stood back from the desk. I said "Otay" and gave her the Little Rascals goodbye wave with my hand under my chin.

෴

With Anne and Avi in Hyde Park. We had walked up Brompton Road through the tourists, past Harrod's, crossing streets until we were under the trees, the summer smell of grass rather than baking cement in the air. Anne was the only one of us wearing shorts, and as we strolled around the narrow end of the Serpentine, the sun shining on the water, joggers passing by, I considered taking off my jeans and lying in the grass in my boxer shorts.

I ended up lying on my back with my jeans on, feeling like a geek, not even able to take my shirt off because I felt too subconscious

FESTIVAL

about it with Anne there. We had circled around to the north side of the Serpentine, lying down where the field slopes gradually towards the sawdust horse track, the cement road for bikers and rollerbladers and then the little marina that rents out rowboats for people to dawdle around in on the water.

Avi was also in pants and a shirt, lying on his side propped up on his left elbow. I was watching a cloud shaped like a human face break up when I heard Avi light a match. I looked over and saw him with a cigarette in his mouth.

Seeing me staring, Avi said "What? I am not eating."

Anne was lying on her back beside me. She raised her head off the ground and looked at Avi. "Avi, did your wife smoke?"

"Your wife!"

"My ex-wife."

"Holy Cow Avi, you never told me you were married."

Avi shrugged, his cigarette idle in his hand. "It was in Morocco when I worked at the newspaper."

"You worked at a newspaper?"

He nodded. "I was a reporter. That is when I began smoking and drinking coffee. It made sitting at the typewriter less boring."

"Avi, how old are you?"

"Twenty eight."

"Geeze Avi, I'm sorry." Avi raised his eyebrows, Anne turned to me, surprise in her eyes. "I mean about…," I waved at them to forget it and lay down in the grass.

"Peter," Avi said, "why did you come to London?"

"For the skiing."

"There is no skiing in England."

"I was misinformed." I paused a second. "You should know that one Avi, you're from Morocco."

"I am even from Casablanca, but it was in Paris that I saw that movie."

"What movie?" Anne asked. She was lying beside me, her sunglasses on, dozing in the sunlight.

"Casablanca."

PART ONE

"Oh." She lay still and silent for a few seconds. "Pete, why did you come to London?"

"Why not?"

"What did you do the last few summers?"

"I found work back home and lived with my parents."

"And your parents told you to buzz off this summer?"

I smiled. "No." I picked a few blades of grass and rolled them between my fingers. I looked out at the boats and sunlight drifting on the Serpentine. "Last summer I felt like I shouldn't be there."

Anne turned her head to me and pushed her sunglasses up onto her forehead, but the sunlight must have been too much for her because she quickly put them back over her eyes. "Why?"

I picked some more grass and tossed the green blades into the air, a hunter checking the wind. I looked at Avi, lying on his back, motionless, his hands clasped across his stomach, then I rubbed my fingers into my eyes, wondering how to explain that the last time I was home I had felt like I was living in an echo of the past.

"It doesn't seem like all that long ago that my family was together, that the posters were still up in my brother and sister's rooms, and my brother and sister were still there. I went home last summer still expecting to feel a part of that family, but I didn't. My brother and sister were gone and my parents were getting used to their empty next. I didn't want to go home again and watch anymore of that life disappear."

Anne sat up and massaged her eyes without taking off her sunglasses. "Why not stay in Toronto?"

"Toronto is nothing more to me than the place where I go to school."

"Don't you have any friends who live there?"

"Most of my university friends are like me – we come from different towns scattered across the province and everybody goes home for the summer."

"But why London?"

"Well I'd never been here before. I spoke the language and could get a job." I looked at the sun, closed my eyes to watch little orange

FESTIVAL

spots race through the darkness, then opened my eyes again. "It seemed like a good place to kill a summer."

Anne looked out at the water, at people stepping tentatively into rowboats along the dock. I lay back the way Avi was, face to the sky hands across my stomach. I saw another cloud formation turn into a human face, a high ghostly face of whites and shades and clefts and valleys, eyes looking down at me. Then slowly the hairline receded, the head began to stretch, the eye sockets lengthened until the last tendrils of billowy flesh separated and the top of the head drifted away, the face gone, splintering into different directions, the sun burning through the smaller clouds that were foolish enough to cross its path.

August 15

Dear Mom:

It is 6:00a.m. Tuesday morning. I called in sick at work. I guess I have some kind of flu – I have a headache and my head is hot, my chest is cold, my back hurts and I have a cough. The hotel doesn't even pay you for sick days, sometimes the maids come to work looking horrible but they can't afford to lose the money.

Anyway, the sun isn't quite up yet, I'm sitting up in bed with my notebook on my lap writing in grey morning light and listening to the classical station on the radio.

I haven't written much this summer so let me tell you now that I've been having a good time. London is a lot more fun than Toronto – it's bigger and the personality of the city changes with every tube stop you get out of. I think perhaps I'm different here as well. I've only lately thought of this and I'm not sure if I can explain what I mean – my eyes seem wider here, I've been smiling more, I've been allowing myself to have fun and I've been with fun people. I don't know, it just seems like the sun has been shining a lot more this summer, seems like I've given life the chance to be exciting for the first time.

PART ONE

The radio is playing back to back Puccini. The humming one from Madame Butterfly just finished and now *O Mio Babbino Caro* is on.

I don't feel up to detailing all my escapades right now. I'll be home in less than a month and I'll tell you anything you want to know when I'm back in Little Falls. Speaking of which, has Dan been up at all? Has the weather been good for gardening? I guess I'll probably only be home for about a week before I go back to Toronto. I wish I had more time. I miss those summer mornings and evenings at the golf course, I miss playing catch in the backyard with Dad and Dan, and I have this funny desire to cut the grass which I imagine Dad will be more than happy to accommodate.

Anyway – another month and I'll be flying home, and then a week or so later I'll have to get on the bus to Toronto. See you soon.

Peter

Tracy Nichols was in her mid 50's. She was plumpish and beginning to show the passage of the years but she wasn't resigned, she was vital, she was active, she was very much alive.

She had her house under control. The bath towels, hand towels and wash cloths all had their assigned place in Tracy's little towel closet. The videotapes stood at attention below the TV, the audio tapes had their little pile beside the tape player.

I found this all very comforting. In highschool I had come across Bob Dylan's quote – *I accept chaos, I'm not sure whether it accepts me* – and found it undeniably cool. But chaos is a dream of the very young who consider themselves overly bound by parents and school etc. When you're actually living chaos it becomes far less interesting.

So in London I entered a well ordered house run by a wonderful woman who cooked my meals for me and allowed me to come and go and act as I pleased, comforted by the simple fact that she was no longer alone in her house.

But I wondered about Tracy. I would come down sometimes in the morning when the phone was quiet, the newspaper still lay outside, the mail hadn't yet arrived, and find Tracy with her back to me, cooking eggs on the stove, the kettle hissing to life for her tea. I'd wonder what she was going to do. She was only in her 50's, she had at least another 30 years to fill somehow, and she had already built one beautiful meaningful life for herself.

What do you do after that? Do you try to build another life? Do you live within memories of your former life?

Before Tracy turned from the stove, before I said "good morning" and announced my presence, I would watch Tracy cooking in the morning light and think of the crossroads she was at, the decision she had to make.

Then I would say "morning Tracy" and she would turn in very faint surprise and say "Oh good morning Peter, fancy some breakfast?"

"That'd be wonderful," and I'd pour the tea for us. My mornings in London with Tracy.

It was ten to three. I was in the staff room getting ready to start the night shift. Sarah came in, saw me and smiled. "Are you working late tonight?"

"Yes maam."

"I'll have to page you all night and keep you on your toes."

I pulled my suspender straps over my shoulders and putting a foot on a chair started to tie my shoelace. "Hey Sarah, do you know a place around here where I could get a sock fairly cheap?"

"Just one sock?"

"Yes."

"Why don't you buy a pair?"

"I don't know, is that the way you buy socks in England?"

"Yes. Don't you buy socks in pairs in Canada?"

PART ONE

"No." I sat down and lifted my left foot up. "This sock was a Christmas present about two years ago, and this one I bought from a Sockmobile on Queen Street in Toronto."

Sarah shook her head and went into the shower room. Mulu entered the staff room being chased by Avi who was teasing her about being late again for her shift. Mulu was one of the maids. She was Moroccan like Avi but her English wasn't as good as Avi's so I only had very brief conversations with her, her smile was bright and spoke the volumes that her faint grasp of English couldn't.

"Peter!" Avi shouted. "You are here, good. I want to go home."

"Long day?"

"Ah," he made a face then remembered something. "Check room 22 tonight. They have a goldfish bowl."

"Really? Did you bring it in?"

"Yes. Very nice man gave me ten pounds."

Mulu knocked on the shower room door and Sarah's voice called out "Just a second!" She came out wearing the black receptionist's dress. She and Mulu said hello then Mulu went into the shower room to put on her uniform.

"I had a goldfish when I was a kid," I said. "One day I decided that he must be thirsty so I poured milk in."

"He died?"

"Yep."

Avi shook his head, chuckling lightly, and Sarah donned that feminine look of sorrow used for trivial things. The only other pet I ever had was a Spaniel that I used to roll around with on the couch, socks stretched between us in games of tug-of-war. She stepped on something and her foot got infected. She died as well.

I became lost I guess because I remember Sarah putting her hand on my shoulder and I looked up not knowing how she got beside me.

"Are you alright?"

༄

FESTIVAL

"That was our stop."

"Right."

"Come." Avi brushed past my legs into the middle of the aisle and pressed the Stop Request button, but the bus rolled on, carrying us further from our destination.

At the next stop I followed Avi out onto the sidewalk, stepping through the piles of sand and wood and fencing where a new drainage system was being installed in the street.

"The restaurant is back," Avi said. "I come usually another way but the building…" and he waved his hands to indicate that the construction on the street had messed up his usual travel plan. We were somewhere in north London but I don't remember where. It was around 8:00pm and we had been drinking since 4:00. Avi had gotten hungry and pulled me away to find a Moroccan restaurant he knew and which he promised was good and cheap.

I think it was called "The Little Prince", or peut-etre "Le Petit Prince", whatever that French children's book is called about the kid who lives all alone on a world which is only a little bigger than he is. When we sat down Avi had his back to the wall and over his head was a mural of a bluish sky and a boy sitting on a smallish earth, a puzzled grin on his face.

Avi ordered us plates and plates of food, asking the English girl who served us what she called each dish, shaking his head and wondering why it wasn't called what he had called it in Morocco.

He prepared my plate for me as my mother would when I was very young. Laying down a bed of couscous, rolling half a kebab onto the couscous then ladling me a bunch of vegetables and the watery sauce the vegetables lay in, then warning me that the sauce I was gleefully dumping onto my food was very hot.

At the Benjamin I had gotten the impression that Avi didn't really eat food. At lunch his meals grew cold on his plate while he smoked and drank coffee. But now I knew why he didn't eat at the Benji, he just didn't like the food.

At this Moroccan restaurant Avi's face beamed as he drank wine, ordered plates of couscous, filled my plate and my glass. Avi should

PART ONE

have been a diplomat, a minor one, the one the government assigns to wine and dine medium level guests – make them happy, forget about pressing policy issues, fill them with a joie de vivre and send them away with nothing but warm thoughts of the country Avi served.

"You and Anne," he said at one point, raising his glass of red wine to his lips.

I looked up at him, at the John Lennon glasses, the short moderately curly dark hair. "Me and Anne what?"

He crossed two fingers together. "Close?"

"No."

"Not no! Yes!"

"Not yes! No! She's insane."

"Insane maybe but she is very happy. It is nice happy people, like sunshine."

I laughed.

"You do not know Inga." This was a statement rather than a question. I shook my head. "She was at the Benjamin for a year. She left when Anne came, Anne took her position I think. Inga and I," the two fingers, "close. She is Swiss. She is in Switzerland now but she writes me very often saying she loves me and she came to London a few times for two or three days only to see me."

He was talking between mouthfuls, the food on his plate steadily disappearing. I was full already and when his hand went up to catch the English girl's attention I inwardly groaned.

"A month ago she sent me her friend who wanted to work in London, and now her friend loves me."

"What do you mean she *sent you her friend?*"

"She lives with me at my flat. She works at Mr. Ferness's other hotel down the street from the Benjamin."

"Did you help her fall in love with you?"

"We sleep together."

I laughed. "What about Inga?"

He shrugged and took a long drink of mineral water, then patted his stomach, or the area where his stomach would be if he wasn't as thin as a stick. "I think it is funny," he said. "Eva, the girl who is here, wrote Inga and said we're in love, so she has broke their friendship over me. Inga called and cried on the phone, and she is coming in two weeks to see if we are really loving. She still wants me."

"Which one do you like?"

He picked up his fork and stirred his couscous lightly. "Inga is very nice. She is smart. She thinks about things. I told her about Mohammed and Cat Stevens and I think she understood."

He worked on his food for several seconds. I had emptied my plate and was delaying helping myself to any more.

"Eva is very beautiful. She drinks and smokes more than I do."

"Really?"

"Yes. It is strange. When we leave a pub I must give her my pint to finish for me because I cannot drink it."

"So which one do you like?"

"Je n'sais pas. I am very happy when I am almost in love with both of them."

He gave me another helping of couscous and vegetables. In Canada I was accustomed to getting drunk and eating pizza, a very solid bread based food that absorbs the alcohol in your gut. In London with Avi I had to eat all these spicy, vegetable based meals, and it always made me feel horrible the next day.

Avi filled my plate and I leaned back from the smooth wooden table. I looked out the front window at people passing on the sidewalk, at the candle which was burning on our table, at the little prince above Avi's head.

"What do you do Peter," as he sprinkled vegetable water onto my food, "when women are fighting over you?"

"Women don't fight over me Avi."

"What do you do when you have to finish with a girl?"

I shook my head. "I haven't broken any hearts either."

He was surprised now. So surprised that he couldn't dig into his food again. "You have not had relationships?"

"Nothing I would call a relationship."

"But girls like you. Anne likes you. She would be with you now."

PART ONE

I took a drink of water and looked up at the little prince alone on his world. I almost opened my mouth to talk about stop signs and glass walls, but I didn't. I caught Avi's eye and shrugged my shoulders. I swept my fork through my food without catching anything.

༄

"What is this?"
"This is the reason we came."
"This?"
"Relax."

A painting at the Tate Gallery, about 9 by 7 feet. It had a horizontal line that divided it into two halves. The top was a light orangish blur, the bottom a blackish red blur. The entire thing was bordered by a hazy strip of brown.

"Have you heard of Mark Rothko?"
"I don't know anything about art, Anne."
"Well this is a Rothko. Should be about mid 1950's."

The gallery was quiet, white light descended on us as we stood about fifteen feet away from the painting.

"What is it supposed to be?"
"It's not supposed to be anything."
"Well that's…"
"Shut up."

I put my hands in my pockets and stood silently beside Anne, bored the way males are bored when their girlfriends drag them into every shop in a mall looking for the right pair of shoes for a pair of jeans that they hadn't even bought yet.

The silence dragged on and it seemed like we had been standing there for ten minutes when I began to wonder what was happening. I looked at Anne's face, her eyebrows narrowed in concentration, she was slightly biting her lower lip, an aura of transfixion about her.

I turned from her face to the painting, the cause of her mood, but as I did she put her fingers to her lips and turned to me. She had the shy sad smile of someone who has been caught leaving a movie with tears in their eyes, and I realized only then that I had been taken there to be moved, that something important had escaped me.

"Well?"

"Anne..."

She looked into my eyes and shook her head. "You're such a hapless geek. That didn't make you feel anything?"

"I wasn't really paying attention."

She rolled her eyes and shook her head. "You know in Star Wars when Yoda says to Luke *your mind is forever in the stars, never on where you are?*

"Yeah."

"Well...," she nodded at me, her eyes wide as though the point she was trying to make was blatantly obvious.

"Is there some kind of symbolic connection between Yoda and Rothko?"

"No, no," she shook her head a smile in her eyes, then stopped as a thought struck her. "Well, maybe."

"Yoda and Grover were done by the same guy you know."

"Do you want to know about this painting?"

"Well you brought me all the way here."

"You have to realize of course that I'm biased. I love modern art."

I shrugged.

She turned from me to gaze again at the two hazy rectangles of colour, the thin border between them, resembling the border between the sea and sky when there are no ships to distract the eye. Anne began speaking slowly, reflectively, the voice of a speaker revealing for the first time ideas which have long been formulating privately.

"This isn't so much a painting as it is an instrument," she said. "Rothko didn't want to show the audience characters feeling emotion, he wanted to provoke emotion in the audience.

"It's religious in a way. He didn't want to create a piece of Catholic propaganda the way Renaissance artists did, he wanted to leave the old ideologies and affect people on a personal level, bring out their personal faith.

PART ONE

"When you look through this gallery you can trace the dissolution of art. How art has broken down into these cryptic designs and shapes. Modern life has broken down as well – religion, the family unit, ethnicity, all of these things are changing, and when you look into this painting you are confronted with the immensity of life, the number of things you don't understand and can't control, the chaos which surrounds us.

"In order to understand the message of this painting you have to put yourself inside it, and in order to be inside this painting, unless you're going to let yourself fall, you have to give yourself something to hold onto, to step on. I put in my family, my friends, my boyfriend from high school, everything which has made me what I am.

"If you look at this painting without building support for yourself, then there is nothing, chaos rules. But if you can build for yourself, if you can prove that when everything else is gone you have the strength within yourself to create a new life, then you can rise above the chaos.

"Rothko is posing a question – do you look at this painting and see everything or nothing? Do you build or fall?"

"What did you see?"

"That's a secret. Stand here awhile. I'm going to wander around."

She walked away, leaving me all alone. The only thing to look at in the painting is the horizontal line racing across the middle, so that's all you look at, and the longer you stare at that line the farther back it seems to stretch, carrying you out of yourself, through time and meaning and reality. You enter an emptiness, chasing a line that divides two nothings, two solitudes.

When Anne's face appeared before me I had to come swimming back into my body, and once back in my body I had a sudden desire to press an anvil into my heart, replace the emptiness with an unbearable heaviness.

I smiled at Anne and flinched my arm out from under her touch. Her hand fell to her side. I turned and tried to force some air back into my lungs.

∽

FESTIVAL

July 10

Dear Hannah:

There's a guy here I've become friends with named Avi. He's Moroccan but he has been in London for two or three years now. He's a porter at my hotel. He taught me the job and we go drinking together a lot.

He is around 28 or 29 years old. He was married for three years in Morocco but the marriage failed, he and his wife split up, and perhaps to escape memories Avi went first to Paris where he has a brother, and then he came to London.

Before I found that he had been married I thought that Avi and I were very much alike – like me he didn't seem to have anything permanent in his life, and he didn't really look like he wanted anything permanent, but that thought has been changing recently. Now I feel that Avi is like me only because he lost something – i.e. he was once better than me.

And what do I mean by *better*? I don't know. Maybe I'm writing because I want you to tell me, because I feel like you're better than me as well.

I wish I didn't have to do this in a letter. I wish I could knock on your bedroom door, hear your voice say *Yes* and walk in and sit on the edge of your bed, watch you push away from the homework on your desk, Simon and Garfunkel on your stereo.

How long ago was that Hannah? Sometimes it seems like yesterday, and sometimes it seems like a whole different lifetime.

Peter

"I think he's more like a guardian angel."
Anne laughed and I took the cap off our bottle of water, offering some to the girls before taking a drink.

PART ONE

"Don't laugh," Sarah said. "If Avi found a child lost in a department store he'd take her hand in his, buy her an ice cream, take her to security and stay right with her, telling her jokes until her parents were found."

"Yeah," Anne said, "but I'd do that, lots of people would do that."

Sarah brushed her hair behind her ear and sat forward in her lawn chair. "But Avi would do it with a grand smile on his face and he'd make you feel like there was nowhere else in the world that he'd rather be than with you at that moment."

I handed Sarah the water bottle and nodded at Anne. "That might be a picture for you kiddo – Avi with a halo."

Anne shrugged, her eyes hidden behind sunglasses. "I should draw Avi sometime, but I don't think I'll beatify him. Maybe I'll just show him holding the hand of a lost child."

Sarah smiled. "That would be nice. If you do it I'll buy it from you."

"Alright," Anne grinned. "Now all I need is a model for my lost child."

I sat forward on my lawn chair, my elbows on my knees, gazing out from under the shade of Anne's patio umbrella at Covent Gardens. We were on the east side of the Market Square, in front of the long, low wall where people sit to rest and eat ice cream, Tuttons Brasserie across the road to our left.

Anne had her easel set up, a few demos of her work on a stand in front of us, but of the five demos, four were modern art (cubes, wavy lines, blurs of various widths and shades) and only one was a portrait, but it wasn't Elvis or Marilyn or someone famous as any other street painter would use to demonstrate his or her talent, it was some girl Anne had seen once for ten seconds in a drug store in Chicago, buying cough syrup for her mom.

Sarah, Anne and I were spending a sunny Saturday afternoon waiting in the Gardens for people to come have Anne draw their picture, but business had been slow, Anne had only done three portraits, and now we were waiting for Avi to show up having finished

FESTIVAL

the day shift, which would be the signal for us to pack up and head to a pub.

Anne picked up her jar of pencils and crayons then ran a hand across the blank, open page of her sketching book, smoothing, straightening wrinkles. "Should I draw him in the nude?" she asked, grinning.

"I wouldn't," I said. "The poor guy will probably be embarrassed enough just having his picture drawn in the first place."

"I turned him a deep blushing red once just by giving him a thank you card," Sarah said, as a smiling pair of lips appeared in grey out of Anne's pencil.

"What'd you give him a thank you card for?" Anne asked, her fingers creating glasses above the lips, a nose supporting the glasses, the oval of a head surrounding the facial features.

Sarah turned her gaze from the passing tourists to Anne's slow magical act of creating something out of nothing, looking up into my interested eyes on the other side of Anne's easel.

"He helped me out once," she said. "I guess it was before either of you started at the Benji." Sarah picked up the water bottle and took a drink, then rubbed her fingers through the perspiration on her forehead. I watched curly hair grow on Avi's head, ears form under the arms of his glasses.

"Some of us, me, Toby, Avi, Inga, who I don't think you two met, and a few other people who have left the hotel, were drinking somewhere, I don't even remember where. I hadn't eaten all day and I was tired and around 10:30 I got sick. I wasn't coherent at all and at that time Avi didn't know where I lived so he left the club with me and took me to his place."

Anne paused in her drawing to look at Sarah. The back of her head was turned to me, so I didn't see the look Anne gave Sarah, but Sarah's answer was "he was a perfect gentleman."

Anne turned back to her easel, noticed me and leaning in towards me she brushed her nose against mine in an Inuit hello. "Smile," she said.

PART ONE

I touched my nose. "You just wiped your sweat all over me."

"He rubbed the small of my back and held my hair behind my neck when I was throwing up in his bathroom, then he put me to bed in his room while he slept on the couch in the sitting room. The next day, which I had off but he didn't, he called in sick so that he could make me coffee and breakfast and take me home on the tube. So..."

"So," Anne interrupted, "he's not the jack-ass I've often said he was."

"No."

Through the people passing before us I caught a glimpse of Avi coming our way from the direction of James Street. I stood up and stepped out from under the umbrella into a dazzling torrent of sunshine. "He's coming Anne, can you finish it up?"

"Most of it. Go slow him up a bit."

I ran through the people and sunlight and heat in my shorts and white T Shirt and coming to Avi put my hands on his shoulders and spun him around to face the opposite direction. "Hey Avi, how was work?"

"Wonderful. Where are we going? Why are you smiling?"

"Anne just finished one of her obscene jokes and you and I are supposed to get ice cream. Il fait chaud."

"You are lucky. I was in a uniform all day going in and out of the sunshine. You could lie out and relax."

"And bake like a chicken."

Avi didn't get that one and gave me a *Pardon?* Look, but it wasn't funny enough to bother explaining. We went to one of the expensive hole in the wall ice cream places in the Market Building and bought four chocolate ice creams with nuts. On our way back, both of us with an ice cream in each hand, I told him that the girls had a surprise for him.

"Anne will buy dinner with her profits?"

"No. We'd be eating French Fries at McDonald's."

Avi shrugged. "I like French Fries." He took a lick/bite of his ice cream and looking at him as we walked along I laughed softly and

FESTIVAL

touched my finger to my nose. "Ice Cream?" he asked. I nodded and he shrugged. We approached the girls in their pool of shadow under the umbrella and Avi sat down in the small chair where Anne's clients were meant to sit.

"Look Avi," Anne said, turning her easel slightly in his direction.

"That's me!" Avi exclaimed, surprised.

"You betcha."

It was Avi looking, and reaching with his right hand, towards something on his right which hadn't been drawn yet. His body was facing straight forward, one foot ahead of the other, Avi caught in mid step as he reached out for an invisible lost child.

"I still need to do some more work on it," Anne said.

"Yes," Avi nodded. "You need to put some ice cream on my nose."

Greenwich Park was a half hour walk from Tracy's house. When I had a day off, or when I was working the late shift, I would get up early and head to Greenwich, trying to arrive before 8:00a.m. I liked the park early in the morning before anyone else arrived. I would wander through the fields, feeling the moisture in the air, alone with the smell of the earth straining to keep its blanket of midnight shadows. It was like being alone in a clearing in Sherwood Forest, your own private world to think and dream in, destiny in your own hands, time left behind in another world that you could almost believe didn't exist.

I would set my knapsack down in the middle of the main field and start kicking around my hackeysack. Alone in a huge green field, dew on the grass, shadows only starting to retreat from the cool morning sunlight, the mist gone but the smell of water still in the air.

I'd stop to pick up my hackeysack sometimes and just stand there, holding the ball in my hand, watching clouds drift by. I guess I was trying to absorb the peace, the timelessness, trying to step

PART ONE

backward into another reality where the silence of the early morning lasts forever.

When people began to arrive, when I no longer felt like the park was mine, and when the grass was more or less dry, I would wander in search of a secluded spot and lie down to read a book or letters from home, or write letters to home. Truth to tell I usually fell asleep, succumbing to a 9:00a.m. nap.

In Greenwich one morning I opened my eyes and there I was – drifting through the blue sky in and out of wandering clouds my arms outstretched like Peter Pan. I smiled, the sun warm on my face the grass tickling cool on the back of my neck. I rubbed my palms into my eyes and sat up to see myself disappear slowly beyond the Observatory.

I've been having a recurring dream about flying since I left high school. In my schoolyard when I was very young we had huge swing sets which we spent recesses flying on, looking out at the other kids playing in the field. During holidays we laughed through long summer evenings twirling on the swings as the shadows stretched out from the forest.

One of the games we played was to start swinging and see who could kick their shoe off the farthest. Another was to swing as high as you dared and see who could jump the farthest. The dream comes from a feeling of weightlessness that those swings gave me, and which I still have a bodily memory of today. There is an instant at the top of your arc when you hover between flight and descent, the small of your back feels like it has been replaced by air, and if you had just one moment more you feel you could fly away. That instant is where the dream comes from.

When you jump off a swing you land feet first then fall forward spilling onto the ground. In my dream I jump, land, but instead of falling I bounce up into the sky and I'm flying – that instantaneous feeling of weightlessness transformed into the power of flight. After all these years I still occasionally find myself carried through the night on the wings of that feeling. I see the Peter Pan from the schoolyard floating through the soft blue evening sky, the green blur of fields

61

FESTIVAL

and forests passing below as I chase the orange haze of sunset leaving behind a trail of night.

That's the dream.

When it came time to leave Greenwich I'd walk out the gates and pass the ice cream stands and antique shops. I'd pass the red double decker buses and circle the Cutty Sark. The biggest boats I had ever seen were sailboats far out on Lake Ontario, so the Cutty Sark was my first meeting with a boat that could actually handle an ocean. It sits in a deep cement hole with the deck three times my height above ground level. There are three main masts standing proud and white with ropes and cords and wires stretching down to the deck. I wished I could have seen it dressed in billowing white sails straining to fly away, but it was dead now, with opening and closing times to see *Long John Silver's Figureheads*, whatever they were. I loved London but sometimes it seemed like the whole city was just one big tourist attraction.

There is a tunnel which runs under the Thames which I would pass, then lean against the railing, looking out at the river. The water seems healthier in Greenwich than it does up by Westminster. It seems greener, more natural. There are no wrecks anchored in the water like floating garbage cans. I'd stand there with my foot up on the lower rail, my arms on the top rail, watching the sun dancing in diamonds on the water.

At Harbourfront in Toronto you lie in the grass or sit on a bench peeking at the water through the people passing on the boardwalk. Children run around playing games behind you, their voices rising and falling in waves of happiness. Seagulls hover high above the lake, dive and emerge from the splash of water without a fish, rising high to circle in the blue sky again.

But I had never found Lake Ontario to be beautiful, and the longer the summer went on, the less interesting I found the Thames.

Once in high school I was camping at a small northern lake near home. No one else had woken. It was April. I was wearing a sweater and my hands were cold unless they were buried in my pockets.

PART ONE

I stood in the quiet of the lake watching wave after wave of sunshine washing onto the shore. I would pick one sunlit diamond after another to follow in from a distance until it vanished silently at my feet.

There was the blue sky the forest the water the sunshine and me. Five nouns and the silence for atmosphere – an image I have preserved in a small glass ball, which I often shake and place in the night above me, watching the snowflakes drift into place lulling me to sleep with thoughts of a different time.

I always left Greenwich regretfully. It was like returning unwillingly to reality.

༺ ༻

I remember a morning when my alarm went off at 6:00a.m., but I was actually working the afternoon shift. When I turned it off I couldn't fall back asleep. I got up, walked past Tracy's closed door, then moved downstairs to the kitchen. I plugged the kettle in and as it hissed to boiling I stood at the counter looking out the window at the pale morning sunlight.

I have a certain affinity for silent moments – they seem truer to me. People hide within silence. I have hidden within silence, but people also hide within words and laughter and music. I think there's more honesty in silence because it doesn't pretend to be anything else.

Once last year at school I woke beside the girl I was more or less seeing. I sat up and swung my legs over the edge of the bed. I thought she was asleep but I felt fingertips touch my lower back, then she sat up beside me, silently. The sun shone in forming a pool at our feet. I took a quarter off my desk and made it disappear in my hands before her eyes. She touched her fingers to my cheek and smiled and I thought of all the things we had said before, and all the things we didn't say then. Silence can be lonely but it can also be everything – that morning's silence meant the touch of her hand on my bare chest, the perfume of her hair in my nose, even remembering how she had

FESTIVAL

taken all the blankets that night, and how she had laughed when I took them back.

Anne asked me once about the girls in my past. I don't remember why, though I'd probably just finished saying something cold and cynical about love and relationships. I tried to shrug the question off, deflect the conversation, but she came back to it.
"You've never been in love, have you?"
"Is it written on my forehead or something?"
"Almost."
"Well, if I was really going to have this conversation I'd first make you define *love*. But since I'm not going to have this conversation I'll just say that yes, you're right, I've never been in love."
"Why not?"
"I really don't want to talk about this."
"I've been in love."
"Yeah and look where that got you." A vulnerable look shot up into her eyes and I prevented myself from finishing with "he dumped you didn't he."
Anne was silent for a few minutes, and now I remember where we were – a bar called Crown Royale in Camden Town. Avi was sitting across the table from us and I remember seeing him put his hand down on a glass of flaming zambucki, then turning his hand over, the glass suctioned to his palm.
"I don't regret it," Anne said. "The breaking up hurt, but I don't regret it."
Some girl I had never seen before sat down beside Avi, his arm slipped around her waist and she laughed, maybe at one of his easy jokes, maybe at his French Moroccan accent. I tipped my glass high into the air and finished my beer, then pushed my chair out a little from the table.
"It's all kind of pointless though, isn't it Anne."
"What?"
"Love. Relationships." This provoked the closest thing I've ever seen to an aghast look. "Well you can't really be in love at our age, can

PART ONE

you? We're all in transit, you say hello then goodbye without having time to do anything more than have sex."

She shook her head at me in disbelief and I smiled. "Not that I'm a remorseless Casanova or anything Anne." I stood up and glanced at the crush of people around the circular bar. "Do you want another beer?"

Anne grabbed my arm and pulled me back down into my chair. "Don't you feel alone?"

I looked at her for a few seconds, then across the table at Avi and his girl, then down at my hands. "I read a book by a guy called Ngugi once. There was a line – *to live and die alone is the ultimate truth*." I raised my head and looked around the bar, then found Anne's eyes again. "I think that's true. I feel alone. Sometimes I wonder if I feel anything but alone."

"That's because you've never loved anything."

"Don't lecture me about this."

"Just promise me something."

"What?"

"Hold onto someone sometime. It makes you feel bigger than you are, like you've touched something universal and timeless simply by touching another person."

"Who should I hold?"

"Hold everyone."

I nodded, giving her an "I'll think about it" look. I spun my empty glass on the table and looked across at Avi whispering something into his girl's ear. I stood up, put my hand on Anne's head and tussled her hair, stepped away from our table towards the crowd around the bar.

HOME

Last Christmas Hannah and Daniel and I were all in Little Falls. Daniel and I were there solo, and Hannah had come from Alberta with her daughter and her husband Bill.

FESTIVAL

One afternoon Mom and Dad and Bill went downtown to do some shopping or something, leaving my brother and sister and I alone in the house where we, or perhaps only I, had grown up. It was like ten years had slipped away except for one thing – the drooling demon in the high chair, Hannah's daughter, my niece.

Daniel and I had to help with a feeding session, and between the two of us I think we ate more strained carrots than she did, Hannah repeatedly cooing "Oh come on honey, look how much Uncle Danny likes it", and rubbing our tummies, licking our lips, grinning our grins we mimed ecstatic enjoyment while our niece wallowed in the delightful spectacle of her two crazy uncles acting like monkeys over something she wouldn't touch with a ten foot pole.

I envy Hannah her family, but I wouldn't want a family. I know I couldn't handle the emotional responsibility. I'm petrified by the thought of someone else's happiness depending on me. I abstain from intimate personal relationships unable to convince myself that I won't weaken some day and run away, leaving someone who was probably too good for me in the first place to mend the tear I'd left in her life. I'm not sure if that's selfish or self-sacrificing.

During that 20 minute meal with my niece I positively revelled in the feeling of being home again with my brother and sister. I went to sleep that night, in my old bed incidentally, the one my body still measures all others by, thinking of how we had all left this house. Being the youngest I was the last to go, and I had to help Hannah and Daniel pack up their belongings. When Hannah went to university out west she rented a U Haul van, we loaded all her stuff in, and then stood in the driveway, Mom, Dad, Daniel and I on a sunny September morning, waving as she slowly backed out onto our quiet, tree-lined side street, looking at her house and family, then waved one last time, pulling away in the van, leaving me to go back into the house, glance at her now bare room, sit down on her bed feeling as though we'd packed her spirit as well.

When Daniel went to Hamilton I inherited some of his clothes and posters, and Dad and I drove him in our truck to Steeltown. We moved his boxes into the house his friends had found, had lunch,

PART ONE

then Daniel stood in his new driveway as Dad and I pulled away, setting off on a very quiet drive through southern Ontario, north on 28, through Peterborough and then the long drive along Highway 7.

For the next three years Hannah and Daniel were distant voices on the other end of the phone – voices which said "Well I'll see you at Thanksgiving/Christmas/Easter, put mom on."

Then I moved out, and having learned that life changes through sending off my brother and sister, I resolved to travel light, so that when change came it would be easy and painless. I never wanted to cry over a half filled box as Hannah had, I never wanted to spend an entire day undecorating a room like Daniel had. I wanted to be a kite, flying high and free, navigating the changes in the wind, trying to sever all the strings that tied me to life and its inherent sorrows.

But I have been a kite for four years now, and I've grown tired of hearing only my own jokes. I look to earth sometimes, wondering if there's anyone holding onto the one string left me, if there's anyone waiting to reel me in.

TORONTO

The corner I like to sit in at Fabulous, away from the front doors, the cashier and most of the tables, isn't exactly what I would call warm. When I settle into one of the high straight backed chairs, my legs and feet, which dangle about a foot from the floor, are warm, but my upper body, the half of me above the counter top, is cold.

Occasionally, even if I'm writing well, I have to drop my pen and warm my fingers around my coffee cup. When I'm writing well though, by the time I notice my fingers, my coffee has grown cold, and being too cheap to spend another loonie on coffee I mutter slightly extravagant curses and start writing again.

What I have here is a notebook I carry under my arm to work, to this café, to my classes and to my apartment. I scribble a memory onto the page, thoughts and images sitting on the ruled lines between

FESTIVAL

two covers. When each memory is documented I close my notebook and trap the memory inside, saying "Farewell, trouble me no more."

But it's not just my memories which fill these pages, and I don't particularly feel like the author of this story. The words of my friends have been copied here practically verbatim, direct from their minds to these pages, my only contribution being the unfortunate selection process of what I can and can't remember.

I've also come to the conclusion that even if this can be declared to be my story, it is really just a retelling of someone else's story, or something else's story.

Everything I've been reading recently seems to have been written with my heart in mind. I'll only namedrop a little: *Now is life very solid or very shifting? I'm haunted by the two contradictions.* Virginia Woolfe. *Why does this generation ask for a sign?* Jesus Christ. *We will never love each other again. We can never see each other again.* Michael Ondaatje.

It seems as though there is a constant repetition of theme within literature, and this has me more or less believing in the "universal story". As I try to exorcise my ghosts I do so with the help of other writers – with Calvino's ancient Indian in South America, Rushdie's *Sea of Stories*, Coetzee's "birthplace".

When I write my last word in this notebook, when I close it and place it in my desk drawer, rubbing the cramp out of my hand, what will I have done? Will I have discovered anything that had been lying hidden?

I doubt it. And I'd be lying if I said I particularly cared.

My life seems to have been spent searching for ingenious ways to trap myself, and this notebook is merely the latest method. When I close it, when I leave these glass walled cafes, at the very least I'll be free. I'll kick open the door to Dylan Thomas's "tower of words", walk over the moat and entering the green fields leave behind this lonely prison where my only company is the alphabet.

The last word in this notebook, the last letter, will, I hope, set me free.

PART ONE

Anne lived in Elephant and Castle, an area I rode through on the 53 when I took the bus into or out of town. The distinguishing landmark in Elephant and Castle, at least for me, was a pub called the Gin Palace. It's huge and very flat, and almost looks like a 1950's Hollywood "build a town" building. It's also a horrendous yellow colour and I wouldn't be surprised if the whole joint glows in the dark. The only reason I could think of for choosing that colour was that the owner thought drunks would be drawn to the glow like moths to a flame.

Anne's flat was in the backstreets. She invited me over for dinner once but I found myself doing all the cooking while she babbled on about Georgia O'Keefe. I had my revenge though. I found a bottle of hot sauce and added it liberally to the tomato sauce, which was meatless since Anne was vegetarian. During the meal Anne didn't say anything, but it took her about six glasses of water to finish one plate of spaghetti.

Anne called in sick two days in a row once. On the second day I finished work at 3:00pm, bought her a USA Today and a package of Chinese instant noodles, and made my way to her flat. One of the Kiwi girls she lived with let me in, and pointing towards Anne's door, whispered "She's in there."

I knocked, a joke ready on my lips, but she didn't answer. I tried again and said "Hey Anne!" She opened the door, motioned to a chair and said "Sit down, I'm almost done." She stood in the middle of the room holding a sketch pad, staring at one of the corners of the room. She flashed the picture at me. It was two walls and a floor meeting.

"I'm going to call it *A Corner of Life*."

"Is that clever?"

She stuck her tongue out, adding a few more touches to the drawing.

"Why don't you add a bunny rabbit or a teddy bear or something?"

"Maybe a mouse hole, give it the hint of a hidden second world."

"I bought you some stuff. I heard you were sick."

FESTIVAL

She shook her head, still drawing. "That was yesterday. And this morning. A little bit earlier this afternoon, but I'm okay now." She looked up, brushing her long hair from her face revealing red, tired eyes. "What'd you bring me?"

I opened my backpack and pulled out the newspaper and the noodles. She grinned, "bitchin gifts dude. How are the Cubs and the White Sox doing?"

"Baseball is boring. Let's go make noodles."

"Let's stay here."

Here was a very small room. Anne was now sitting cross legged on her narrow bed. I was on a chair between the bed and the window, a dresser with a mirror on the wall across from me. The walls bore pages from the Tribune, O'Keefe prints in pinks, white and blues, party hats which she must have picked up at Christmas and Fourth of July parties, and the two quotes, each of which she had printed out very plainly by hand on clear white paper.

The first was *Mad with a completely physical realization of the origins of life bliss.* The other one was *He had a tattoo on his arm which said BABY, and another one that just said HEY.* Jack Kerouac and Jim Croce – the irreverent mind of Anne.

But she wasn't the life with no regrets girl now. She moved without her usual energy, her eyes weren't sparkling, she wasn't baiting me or hitting me, and although the window was open it must have just been opened, for the beautiful day outside hadn't affected the stuffiness of the room.

The pencil stopped dashing across the sketch pad, she gave up pretending she was busy. She lay down on her side, facing me and the window. She closed her eyes.

I put the paper and noodles on the bed beside Anne. I looked out at the blue afternoon sky. I let silence hold onto us for a few minutes before turning back to her. "You haven't been locked in here for two days straight have you?"

"I went to the bathroom a couple of times."

"And you haven't eaten anything?"

"Haven't felt all that hungry."

PART ONE

I sat down in the chair beside the bed, leaned forward, elbows on my knees, my hands clasped together. Call in sick and lock yourself in your room for two days. That's interesting.

"I know what you're thinking," she said, opening her eyes.

"I hate when you use that big brain of yours to read my mind."

"You're thinking that I must be incredibly weak."

"No." I found her eyes, the shower of hair on the pillow. "You're one of the strongest people I've ever met."

"Oh bull."

"What happened?"

"HA!" Anne burst out with this sometimes. I think for her it means something like "Holy Cow! This is such a crazy story you'll never believe it!"

She sat up, adjusted her pillow against the headboard of the bed and sat with her back to the wall. She was wearing shorts and a white T Shirt, and as she crossed her legs beneath her she brushed the hair from her face, perhaps so that she could see me out of the corner of her eye.

"Do you ever feel that you spend every day pretending to be strong, stable, emotionally secure, and that sometimes the act becomes unbearable and you have to let yourself break down?"

I shook my head slightly. "No. I don't know."

"When I got back from work on Monday I came in here and fell apart. I pulled the blind down, turned off the light and curled up in a ball on the bed. I told myself that I had no friends, no one who loved me and I just lay here until I fell asleep." She cast me a look, perhaps pausing to allow me to say something, but feeling out of my depth I kept silent.

"I still didn't feel like going outside yesterday, so I called in sick. I called in sick today as well. But I've been healing today. I made a cup of coffee. I changed the clothes I'd been sleeping in. Tomorrow I'll get back out on the streets, go to work, and I'll wonder if I really pulled myself together again, and the answer will be yes – not in the sense that I'm not broken, that I was mentally able to glue the thousand different strifes and emotions of Anne together again, but rather that I took the only option."

"Which is?"

She rubbed her hands along her knees, she clasped and held the soles of her feet. "You build again."

She made it sound so easy, so natural, that I smiled. "How do you do that Anne? Say Abracadabra?"

She stood up and moved to the window, breathing in the summer air. She lifted her arms and hands into the air, stretching her back, going up onto tiptoes, seemingly reaching for the ceiling, a yawning squeal escaping her mouth. "I guess I thought about who I am, who I've been, who I want to be. If you can figure all that out you can piece yourself back together whenever you need to."

She turned to me, smiling, and I noticed that mischievous grin was back in her eyes. She stepped to the bed and picked up the chicken noodle soup, then she leaned close to me and touched her lips to mine, her tongue searching for an opening. After a few seconds I pulled away.

"Anne."

"Pete?"

"Let's not start anything here that we can't finish."

TORONTO

I don't dislike them, but at the same time I don't particularly like children. I do however like the thought of them.

When I work the morning shift I'm heading east on College Street from about 8:20am to 8:40am, and in Canada this is when children trudge reluctantly to school. On College therefore I've come to recognize the kids that I pass three or four times a week, me to work them to school, neither of us wanting to go where we're going.

As the autumn has progressed into winter, as the mornings have become colder, the clothes the kids wear has changed. At first it was

PART ONE

light summer jackets, sometimes only a pullover. Now scarves have appeared, wrapped conscientiously around some of the kids' necks, dangling from the pockets of the more rebellious ones, dragging along the sidewalk behind the sloppy ones who couldn't care less.

While I don't really enjoy talking to children, and wouldn't want to be trapped in an elevator with them, they still make you smile. Not because of some endearing childish lisp or habit or outburst, but because children are the way humanity replenishes optimism.

The joke in my family had been that after waiting for four years to conclude that Daniel and Hannah were idiots, my parents tried again with me. This isn't just a family joke though, humanity's answer to the mistakes of modern history is to look into the distance and mutter *Tomorrow* – believing the only thing there is to believe, that somehow tomorrow will be better, the children will make it right. The pessimists will probably say that this is exactly the problem, the responsibility for making the right decisions is continually put on the shoulders of future generations.

BUT – I'm not juggling all these thoughts when I walk to work in the morning. I'm usually pleased enough simply to be walking in the right direction, making the right turns. It just cheers me slightly, more than the Matisse that Anne recommended, to see some kid trundling along like a walking package that his or her mother wrapped up, kicking at a stone or a chunk of ice every 4th or 5th step like I did when I was young, like my brother did, my father, my grandfathers.

I feel proud of something, like I should change my resume, the first line declaring – "In the winters when I was a kid I used to walk down the street kicking chunks of ice and karate chopping snowbanks with my hockey stick – HIRE ME!"

❧

At lunchtime the cook would fix something up and everyone working the day shift had a half hour break to eat in the staff room. Toby usually made us something good, like fish and chips, or chicken burgers, or potatoes and beef, but Toby was only one of the cooks.

FESTIVAL

There was Pamela, a big hearty lady from Jamaica who was about thirty. She had a great laugh and a great need to grab the various males she worked with, like Avi and me, and give us great smothering hugs. Anyway, I followed Avi into the staff room once, carrying a plate of Pam's unidentifiable green and red and yellow vegetables covered with a thick orange-brown broth.

The staff room was already full. The table was only big enough for two people on each side. Mulu and Ruth were together on one side, Pam and Anne were at the end near the window, and Jen was on the third side. Avi and I put our plates down on the side near the staff room door.

Richard came in just after us, heading for the small storeroom where the wine and the liquor and beer were kept. Richard was the head porter, the man who had hired me. He was short and thin with his receding hair cut down to stubble-length. He opened the storeroom on the far wall and picked out two bottles of wine. He locked the door then came back around the table stopping when he saw Mulu nibbling on a raisin biscuit. He smiled, a bottle of wine in each hand. The raisin biscuits were not for the staff to eat. We could have anything except alcohol and raisin biscuits. I didn't care that much so I never asked why, though I guess they were difficult, or expensive, to make.

"Mulu, where did you get that?"

"Room 6 they not eat."

"A guest in room 6 ordered them and didn't eat them?"

Mulu nodded and Richard thought a second. "Mulu, there is no room 6."

"Room 54."

"Room 54 doesn't exist either." He shook his head and looked up at the ceiling in resignation. "Mulu, no raisin biscuits," he said, shaking his finger at her, as he left.

Mulu finished the biscuit with a happy grin on her face. I watched her for a few seconds, laughing at the way she was glowing. I looked down at my plate, stabbed another anonymous chunk of

PART ONE

vegetable, and waved Avi's smoke away from me. I pushed back from the table putting my plate in my lap.

"I can't believe you do that."

"What?"

"Smoke and eat at the same time. That's just plain weird."

He inhaled deeply then blew smoke up towards the ceiling. "It is the same," he said. "I have not tasted food since Morocco."

"God, your guts must just be disgusting."

Jen made a face. "Peter…"

"Come on Jen – remember seeing those X Ray shots in highschool of smokers' lungs? That's Avi."

"I know what you mean, but it is lunchtime."

"What are guts?" Avi asked.

"Your insides. Your stomach."

"My stomach is not disgusting."

"Why don't you quit smoking so that you can taste beer again?"

"What Peter, I like smoking. When you are at a pub women come to you and ask you for a light."

"Can't you just carry a lighter?"

"But if you are not smoking they will not think that you have a light."

"You're a trouser snake Avi," Anne sighed.

Avi looked at her. "What is that?"

Anne laughed.

Avi's plate was on the table before him, the food barely touched. He was wearing his pop bottle glasses, the smoke from his cigarette drifting up past his face. He was grinning and staring across the table at Anne, who was chuckling to herself.

I stabbed my fork into some vegetable and as I chewed decided from the texture that it was a potato. I looked at Anne laughing at Avi, at Mulu and Ruth and Jen eating hungrily, having worked harder than the rest of us, at Pam who I barely knew and at Avi who I thought I knew very well. I felt at home.

FESTIVAL

I clattered down the stairs. I had slept late and had to hurry to be on time for work. At the bottom of the stairs through the open kitchen doorway I saw Tracy with her back to me, cooking something on the stove. "Tracy, morning. I'm late for work I'll see you later."

She turned as I babbled and when I moved towards the front door she called out "But you haven't eaten yet!"

I unbolted the front door and turned to her standing behind me in the hall. "I'll grab something at work."

She held a finger up to me. "Just a minute." She dashed into the kitchen and came back with an apple. "Can't let all this fruit go to waste."

I took it and smiled. "What will you do Tracy, when I go? I only have about two weeks left now."

"Oh try to get another boarder I expect. Toby might have other homeless friends."

I nodded. "Well, I gotta go, thanks for the apple." I stepped outside, through the very small front garden, and turned left along the walkway that took you past the long row of attached houses towards Amersham Vale, the street that led up to the rail station.

I slung my backpack over my shoulders and taking a bite out of the apple thought of Tracy holding her finger up and disappearing into the kitchen, and then of the crossroads I saw Tracy as being at – a woman alone after having raised a family, a woman whose children were now grown and raising young families themselves, a woman faced with a future of reflection or a future spent trying to forge another life.

What would she do?

If you believed Anne there was only one choice, and maybe, especially for Tracy, this was true. As a child Tracy had been evacuated from London because of the war. She was a member of a generation that had been taught at a young age the value and frailty of life. Tracy might not think twice about filling her house with boarders, maybe even falling in love again if the opportunity arose. How else would she whittle away the loneliness? How else would she avoid T.S. Eliot's fear of a handful of dust?

PART ONE

At night Harrod's is lit up like a giant yellow Christmas Tree, thousands of lights shining in the darkness. Once in a while when I finished the late shift I'd walk up the street to the Knightsbridge tube, which was less convenient than South Ken, just to see the lights. I remember leaning against the windows in one of the hotel rooms one night, Jen buzzing around behind me doing the turndown. Jen was from French Montreal. She was pretty and sweet with a Quebecois accent that simply charmed me. She was in London on a student work program, going into her second year at the University of Ottawa in September.

She asked me twice, but it was only as her voice trailed away the second time that I realized I had heard her the first time. "What are you looking at?"

I turned from the window, the pale view of the Brompton Oratory in the darkness. Jen was pulling the thick bedspread off the bed, folding it at the foot of the bed. "Nothing. I was just thinking that the lights would be on now, up at Harrod's."

Jen stashed the bedspread out of sight behind a chair. "I wish I was a porter," she said. "Drink coffee in the kitchen all day, walk around bothering the maids at night, very good job."

I stayed where I was, standing next to the window, bored, nothing really to do unless the front desk paged me on my beeper. Jen leaned over the bed and tucked the sheets and blanket back into half a V shape, then raced over to the other side of the bed, pulled the sheets back and made a whole V.

I moved from the window, turned on the two shaded bedside lamps and turned out the main ceiling light. I sat down in a chair on a pair of pants which I hadn't noticed. I stood up and carefully moved them, then collapsed back into the chair. Jen paused in her bustling with her clean towels and her rubbish bag to stop in front of me. She raised her chin slightly and said "Qu est-ce qu'il y a?"

I shrugged and smiled in the half light. Jen shook her head, a faint smile in her eyes as she began to bustle again. I rubbed my palms

FESTIVAL

into my eyes, from the darkness I heard a beautifully slightly accented voice softly repeat my name – *Peter, Peter, Peter.*

──────

I was sleeping, listening to waves lap at a shore, when I heard my name whispered through my dreams.

"What?" I muttered, half asleep, opening my tired eyes to the moonlight shining on my bare arm.

"Peter."

"What?"

"I'm running across the river."

I jumped up and started running. I was running through a sunny field when a wall of darkness rose infinite ahead of me. I sped inside and saw white flashes of feet and foam as someone ran across a river. I ran into the water up to my waist but my heart grew cold and the mud grabbed at my feet.

"Peter!"

"I can't see you! I can't get across!"

No one answered. A wind began to blow cold along the river, dancing with the dark trees on the far shore. I ran my hand across the surface of the water as though it were a pane of glass, then turned and staggered back up the bank. I sat down in the sand and looked out over the river, running my hand through my hair in desperation.

──────

"So Peter…"

A voice behind me, not a voice that would make one see angels, but a nice voice, warm, a friend's voice.

"Anne."

"I bought you a Molson Canadian." Her hand appeared, setting the glass down before me on the table. As her fingers drifted away I replaced them with mine. If it was India in the 1950's we could sip from a shared cup and be making love.

PART ONE

She set her own glass down and sat across from me. A friend's voice?

"How long do you have now?"

"Next Saturday."

"Are you going to work right up till then?"

"I told Richard and Mr. Phipps that my last day would be Thursday."

She nodded and took a drink of beer. Behind her, out of the open doors of the Maple Leaf, dust was swirling in the sunlight like snowflakes in a storm.

"Did you say goodbye to Jen when she left?"

"Yes." Yes. I had said goodbye to Jen.

※

"Have you said goodbye to Avi?" I asked.

"Yes, and Mr. Phipps."

"Phipps! What did you say to him?"

"Oh he likes me. He said good luck."

Jen pulled a pen and a notebook out of her locker. "Peter can you write your address down for me? I would like to write you."

"I can give you my home address. I don't know my address at school yet."

"Your parents can send you my letters?"

I nodded as I wrote. When I finished she handed me a slip of paper. "That is my address, I would like you to write me also."

I smiled and prevented myself from saying anything caustic and bitter about the pointlessness of our bothering to keep in touch. "Which direction are you going Jen?"

"The Knightsbridge Underground."

"I have to go to the post office across from Harrod's. I'll walk with you."

We left the staff room, turning right into the short hall that led to the staff entrance. Jen opened the door, holding it for me as

FESTIVAL

we stepped outside, It swung slowly closed as I followed Jen up the staircase onto the street.

Brompton Road was shining in the sunlight. I tried to walk beside Jen but we were zigzagging through the crowd and I ended up following along behind her most of the time. She had her hair in a long pony tail, her backpack on her right shoulder. I loped along behind her losing touch with everyone else around me. I was lost in the bouncing of her hair and if she had kept walking I could have followed her through Europe and back home just as easily as I was drifting behind her in the sunshine and crush of Brompton Road.

She eventually stopped and turned to me. "The tube is over there." She pointed across the street where Harrod's stood proud and decadent. We had already passed the first entrance to the tube. The other one was slightly farther up the road. "I'm going to cross," she said, stepping close and hugging me. I clumsily put my arms around her waist.

"How do you say goodbye?" I asked.

"Au revoir. You know that."

"No, really goodbye."

She paused, then squeezed me and stepped away. "A Dieu."

"Jen..," I began but I didn't know what to say, how to prevent her from disappearing. "Be well."

She looked away. I watched her search for words as cars passed behind her, glittering in the sunlight. Tourists peered in the display windows of Harrod's, flags fluttered above the entrance, the doorman dressed in green opened the door of a black cab. Jen looked into my eyes. "Peter, I would check the schedule this summer, to see when we would work together. I knew if you were there it would be good, fun. I think I will smile, when I remember you."

She hugged me, and then crossed the street. She headed along past Harrod's in the same direction we had been walking before. I watched her from my side of the street and followed along across from her. She started to get mixed up in the swirl of tourists and I began to lose her. I caught her pony tail bouncing above a white T

PART ONE

Shirt, then I saw only her hair, then nothing. I stopped walking and stared across the street, oblivious to the people jostling me, the traffic on the road, the sunlight in my eyes.

Tiny snowflakes.

❦

"She said she would think of me and smile."

Anne nodded. "I'll probably think of you and smile. You're funny looking."

"What bothers me is how pointless it was getting to know Jen when two months later we had to say goodbye."

"You're not supposed to think of that, duckboy. Live for the present. Carpe Diem. Carpe Castore."

"I don't even know what the present is."

"The present is the beautiful girl you're drinking beer with at the Maple Leaf."

"Would you understand if I said that that mischievous grin of yours is hazy and I'm looking at you as if you're already gone?"

Anne shook her head slightly. I looked down from her eyes and started tracing figure eights on the table. "From one day to the next I don't know whether to smile at what is good in life, or cry at how fast it fades away."

"So where does that leave you?"

"Leaves me pounding on the wall between my life and real life."

Anne picked up my pint glass and nonchalantly poured beer onto my hand and onto the table. Since it was Anne it didn't surprise me.

"What was that for?"

"For being a self indulgent little prick. If that wall exists it's of your own creation."

❦

FESTIVAL

July 23

Dear Pete:

I could write pages and pages for you, but I won't, mainly because you already know the answer.

1. Read *Room With a View* again.
2. If you aren't happy now, when were you happy? At home 10 years ago with me and Dan and mom and dad? If you were happy being a member of a family, and you can't go back to our old one, what do you have to do? What have I done? What did your friend Avi try to do?

You're waiting for someone to pull back an enormous curtain and yell "Look! This is Life!" but it won't happen. Meanwhile life is happening in all these crooks and corners around you and you don't notice.

Stick your hands in, Pete. Go to the beach and stick your hands into the sand, then lift them up and grieve over the sand that slips between your fingers but hold onto as much as you can and even if you lose everything at least you tried, at least your hands are dirty, at least for those minutes or months or years you had something to care about.

The greatest sin should be a life lived with clean hands.

Hannah
Calgary

PART ONE

TORONTO

My friend in Toronto, the girl whose fingers slid through my hair the night of our party, she inspired a few lines once:

A tear running down your cheek
Made me wonder what it was all about.
I never understood that it was life,
And that life was something worth crying about.

I met her at a few movie theatres, we drank coffee at a few Maison de Croissantes. I taught her how to lick the salt, chew the lemon and throw the tequila over her shoulder, and she taught me how to inhale cigarette smoke so that it burns your lungs.

She seduced me one night. A bunch of us had gotten drunk at the Red Raven and then she invited us all back to her place at the College. At 1:30a.m. people were rising and leaving, others were asleep in their chairs. She made me tea and brought me Dad's Oatmeal Cookies. I smiled. I must have told her about oatmeal cookies once, or maybe she just noticed that they were the only food I kept regularly in stock.

Anyway, I sat on her couch with my tea and cookies, and she sat beside me, helping me when I tried to dip my cookie into my tea but missed. The next morning I woke up beside her.

It was about 6:30 or 7:00 a.m., my internal alarm clock was still working. I took a few moments to figure out where I was, a few more to find my clothes, and then I left.

She called me for a few weeks, but I would just listen and make non-committal grunts. A month passed and then she cornered me in the Syd Smith building after Quebec Politics, asking me to go to Diablo's with her for coffee.

She asked me what kind of twisted jerk I was. This struck me as kind of funny and I just smiled.

She told me how much she liked me. I told her I liked her quite a bit as well.

FESTIVAL

In the end I walked her home, and in a halo of streetlight outside her house I told her that I didn't believe in love, not yet.

She asked when.

I said "maybe soon" and her head lolled onto one side, her eyes narrowed in concentration, trying, it appeared, to see into my skull and discern what was rolling around in there.

I stepped forward, put my hands on her shoulders and kissed her on the forehead.

"Peter?"

"Yeah?"

"*Soon* better not be too long."

I nodded, smiling. "No." I took a few steps backward, my feet brushing a few leaves that still remained from the fall. I turned and my footsteps fell on another dark street, retreating from life one final time. *Soon* was only a matter of pages, of a few final ghosts.

꩜

At Covent Gardens Anne led me off the train. Jen stayed behind and I stood on the platform looking at her through the window. She waved at me through the glass. I stepped towards her my mouth slightly open but the train began speeding away. I stood silent for a few seconds before I noticed Anne near me. "Where is Jen going?"

Anne punched my shoulder and grabbing my shirt tugged me towards the lifts to the surface. "She's going home and we're going to Avi's bar. Haven't you been listening?"

"My mind wanders when you start babbling."

She hit me again and Avi, who was strolling ahead of us, laughed at me. "Peter, Peter, you are drunk."

"You're not?"

"Oh I am drunk but you are also drunk."

We stepped out of the station and headed down James Street. The light had broken and people were beginning to leave for the night. Avi kept strolling ahead of me and Anne. I looked longingly at the white wooden hut where a guy made crepes and donuts in a deep

PART ONE

fryer. I loved his donuts and I was about to move towards the hut but Anne tugged my arm and I had to keep following along behind her.

In front of the Rock Garden several people were still dining at the tables, a bunch of people were sitting along the wall of the market building, watching the tenor sax player who had apparently just finished a song. He lit a cigarette as people clapped for him. "Don't clap," he called out, "throw money." His dog was chasing after a ball that a drunk in shabby clothes was tossing around. The drunk seemed like a dusty London pigeon, his elbows high at his sides, one foot in the air, delightedly watching the dog scurrying around at his feet.

Avi turned left at the market building and Anne led me left as well. The craft stalls were deserted, the merchandise gone as were the curtains that the merchants hung to form walls between their goods and the goods of the person at their side. A man with a hose was spraying water on the cement floor, laughing with a friend beside him as the remains of the day's trading washed away.

"Anne where are we going?"

"Brahms and Liszt."

A large bald man appeared out of the darkness, rushing towards us. He had a kit of threads and scissors in his hand, one of the last hair-tiers still working the night. He and I both spun as we passed. He gazed longingly at Anne's long hair, then glanced at his watch. "The wife's going to kill me."

Inside the market building the long aisles of wooden cabinets where merchants displayed their figurines, hats, clocks, mirrors, crafts, quilts, clothing were folded and locked up, an unarmed security guard was wandering bored amongst them, a walkie-talkie babbling softly at his side.

As we passed Tuttons Brasserie the Gardens was quiet enough that I could hear the tinkling of glasses and distinguish different conversations. Waiters in red and white were hovering around, waiting for the night to end. If it had been up to me we would have taken a table there and ordered coffee, but it wasn't up to me and at Brahms and Liszt I handed two pounds to a resplendently ugly doorman then followed Avi down some stairs. He moved off somewhere into the darkness and Anne and I took a table. The place felt like a basement. A dirty basement with leaky pipes. A band started to assemble against the wall across the room from us. Avi came strolling to our table with three glasses and two bottles of wine.

"I thought you were drunk," Anne said.

He shrugged and crinkled his nose. "This is only wine. I buy wine to become sober." He poured us each a glass and we touched them together. The band started playing something horrible. It sounded like Hendrix doing the Sesame Street theme song. Avi reached across the table and tapped my arm. "There is a dance floor for you! Music! Why do you sit down?"

I looked at him. He had put on his shaded glasses and there wasn't enough light to read by. "This isn't exactly what I would call dancing music."

"No?" He finished off his wine and stood up. "I will dance." He weaved through the mostly empty tables around us, reached the narrow aisle and walked to the open patch of cement in front of the band. There he started shuffling, moving nothing but his feet, and his feet seemingly oblivious to the music the band was playing.

Anne stood up and followed Avi's path to the dance floor. While Avi stepped slowly and politely, his hands clasped behind his back like a slightly drunk diplomat at a government function, Anne began stomping and jumping trying to make sense of the horribly clashing chords of the music through the movement of her body. I sat there drinking my wine, smiling. Anne and Avi seemed to be filling the entire room with their energy, their personalities. The other people in the basement were all dropping into their glasses.

The Hendrix-Sesame Street song ended and the band started an upbeat Beatles tune. I stood up and wound my way past the tables to the dance floor. Avi was still moving to his inner music but I decided to dance to the band. The three of us bopped around by ourselves for two or three songs and then other people started dancing. The floor eventually became crowded and Avi went back to the table and sipped his wine.

PART ONE

The band started playing some grunge stuff and a punk with a huge mane of black dreadlocks started moshing around. When he came near me I bounced into him and we both fell backwards, me towards a wall and him into the crowd of dancers.

I moved back into the crowd where three or four punks were now moshing around. I got up beside them and started to jump into and against them. The huge guy with the dreadlocks spotted me again and bounced me into the wall. My back hit first, then my head flew back and cracked against the perspiring cement of the wall. I slumped down, trying to keep my knees from buckling, trying to focus again, the dance floor having transformed into the blur of an impressionist paint stroke.

When I was able to focus I looked through the periphery of half-hearted dancers into the core of the floor where Anne was swirling and jumping and thrashing beside the guy with the dreadlocks and the other moshers who appeared to be his friends. Anne had her back to them, facing me but not seeing me, a grinding sort of fury on her face. The dancing of a tall blond mosher made him land for a millisecond with his face directly above Anne's head, the two of them facing me like a two headed monster.

Anne jumped and threw her head back, smashing the blond guy's nose in a crunch of bone that I'm sure I heard leaning dizzily against the wall.

Anne stepped away, raising her hand to her head, and turning saw the blond guy put a hand to his nose to stem the bleeding. He turned and tripped quickly through the dancers towards the other corner of the basement.

Anne watched him leave, then walked towards me rubbing her head. "Are you okay?" she shouted. I nodded and she took my arm, pulling me back to our table.

As were moving through the first set of tables she stopped and stared at a man who was sitting by himself. He grinned up at her, a leering look on his face. She grabbed his nose and shook it and his head around. When she let go he stared up at her more surprised than

FESTIVAL

angry and said "okay love, sorry." Anne found me again and resumed leading me to our table.

"What was that for?" I asked as we sat down.

"Didn't you see what he did?"

"No."

"He groped my leg the horny bastard."

"Really?" I looked back through the gloom of the bar. He was still sitting there, watching people dance. "Do you want me to go back and do something?"

"No, no. I took care of him."

Avi refilled Anne's glass, emptying the first bottle. He opened the second one and filled my glass. "What do you think?"

"Of this place?" I asked, and Avi nodded. "It needs more heat, better music and fewer punk jerks."

"It is good though," Avi said, waving his hand, "the atmosphere."

We rolled out of Brahms and Liszt Avi with his hands in his pockets Anne talking excitedly about something and me with my head in the sky. We had to get to the Trafalgar Square night buses now. As we walked through Covent Gardens I was looking up at the sky but when I realized that all I was seeing was smog and clouds I lowered my head. I moved away from Avi and Anne and jumped over a rubbish bin. I spotted a waist high parking barrier ahead of us so I started running and tried to hurdle it but I didn't clear it. I twisted in the air and landed badly on one foot, almost falling.

"Pete," Anne called, "you're not going to make the Olympics doing that."

"I must be drunk or something."

"Or dizzy," Avi said, chuckling. "You were dancing with walls tonight." I turned to him and he grinned at me. "That one with the hair, he was big."

He started laughing and put a hand on my shoulder. Anne took my open hand in hers.

PART ONE

Avi led us to Trafalgar Square where he wandered around and then stopped, planting himself to a piece of pavement. I opened my eyes like a child who has woken from a deep sleep in the back of a car, realizing that the car had stopped moving and wondering where we were.

"Where is your bus Avi?" Anne asked.

He yawned and pointed at his feet. "It will be right here."

It was very late now. Red double decker buses were parked around the Square, people in scattered groups were waiting to board the buses that would take them home. I looked down at the still fountains and the lions and Nelson's Column and yawning I almost fell down. I hadn't drunk so much or been up so late all summer and I felt it as a weakness in my legs and a dis-orientation in my mind. I saw grey shapes flitting around the fountains in the night.

I heard my name called as though someone waking me from a dream. I turned to Avi and he pointed behind me. Anne was across the road, down from us, near the Canadian Consulate. She had shouted to me while standing in front of a parked bus. She waved then stepped inside and I started walking towards her. She appeared on the upper level and waved through the glass as the bus began moving.

I turned back to Avi who was standing straight his hands in his pockets at his bus stop. I walked back to him and he asked me which bus I was taking.

"The 53."

He looked at me, expressionless, then looked at Anne's bus, which was turning a corner in the darkness at the far side of the Square. "That is the bus Anne is on."

I looked across the Square as my bus vanished. "Oh."

"You have to wait one hour. Do you want to stay at my flat?"

I shook my head to say no, then shook it vigorously to wake myself up. I patted Avi's shoulder and motioned goodnight to him. I started running.

FESTIVAL

I ran around the Square, across the street along the Strand turning at Charing Cross onto the road that leads down to the Embankment Station. I jumped over one sleeping bag then another then stopped, shook my head, and started running again.

The Embankment Station was closed so I clambered over one fence into the small park beside the station then over another fence onto Embankment Road. I saw Cleopatra's Needle and stopped. I turned from it running west along the river along the sidewalk under Charing Cross bridge past the Tattershall Steamer alongside strings of yellow lights being passed by speeding cars and passing dead hulking boats anchored out on the river.

I found myself in the air. I don't know if I tripped or if I jumped but I was in the air, in slow motion, starting to stretch my arms as though I might fly for a second before I fell.

I crashed down onto the stone walkway on top of a chalk painting. It was beautiful, almost glowing in the darkness. It was like a stained glass window had been left out on the sidewalk in the night.

I hit with my chest first, then my face slapped down on the hard stones. I slowly turned to the painting and found myself looking at a beautiful girl's face. I sat up. It was a woman with wings, an angel playing a harp disappearing into a dark purple background.

I stood up shakily, drunk and almost unconscious. I put my hands on the cement wall, looking out at the Thames. A breeze appeared out of the night, fingering the string of yellow lights above me, rustling the leaves of the trees behind me. I pressed my face into my hands, rubbing my eyes, then laid my hands flat on top of the cement wall, watching the river run, drifting with the wind.

⁂

Sometimes the Thames truly mesmerized me. I would stand on Westminster Bridge leaning over the railing facing east towards St. Paul's. The traffic would pass along the Embankment, people would move on the walkway behind me. I would gaze at the Eagle atop the

PART ONE

War Memorial, listen to the trains passing on Charing Cross bridge, watch the blue sky turn grey.

I would just watch the Thames, flowing below me, reminding me, as rivers and stars always do, of the brevity of human life. Staring down at the water, pondering time and rivers and life would bring me to Virginia Woolfe. I imagine her gathering the stones, putting them into her pockets, pausing for a second at the river's edge before starting her last walk.

I picture her head dropping down below the surface of the water, the life within her panicking, trying to cough water out of her lungs, but her mind, perhaps, at peace - knowing that her own hands had gathered the stones, her own feet had carried her to the water.

Virginia Woolfe then, who embraced death, would be counterpointed with Terry Fox, who would have dove into the water to save her. Virginia's choice of death intrigues me, but so does Terry's struggle for life. What drove him? How do you enjoy life enough to fight for it when every breath is a minor war? How do you run along the Trans Canada Highway, feeling the cancer creeping through you, stealing what you so desperately want to hold, and still smile at the landscape, still think that life, even this life, is good? How do you run a Marathon of Hope and say *Somewhere the pain has to end*. How do you believe that the pain will end so fervently that you make others believe?

I had a dream once, just before I travelled to London. I saw myself walking up our side street back home in a thunderstorm. I wasn't hurrying, I was just ambling along in the rain. I went up to our front door and tried my key but it wouldn't go in the lock. I tried a few times then stood there, staring down at my keys in my hand, rain pattering in my palm.

I knocked on the front door and my mother answered. She said "Yes can I help you?" without recognizing me. I said "Mom, it's Peter," but she shook her head with a sad look in her eyes. "I'm sorry, I don't know a Peter." She closed the door and dazedly I walked back out onto the street, into the stormy darkness, and sitting down in

FESTIVAL

the middle of the road I wrapped my arms around myself, the rain streaming through my hair and down my face.

That dream woke me up and I sat on the edge of my bed freezing and crying, finally realizing that I should call home before doing anything rash.

༺༻

My favourite room in the hotel was on the second floor. It has a high ceiling and tall windows making up the far wall. The thick carpet and the walls were cream coloured, the curtains maroon. The closet door and the room door were deep dark brown. The bed stood slightly under waist level, supported by four wooden pillars that continued up to support the canopy which floated five feet above the bed. A thick duvet, which the evening room attendant would remove when he or she did the turndown, covered the bed. Four dark pink cushions of two different sizes were arranged in a diamond at the head of the bed.

The room looked through a wall of windows at the large English garden from which the area "Benjamin Gardens" took its name. There were two sets of doors within the windows which could be opened to let the breeze wash through the room. I remember entering the room near the end of the summer to do the minibar. The doors in the windows were open, the summer smell of green grass and warm air sweeping towards me.

I stood looking out at the garden, the sunshine, the peace, then moved to the closet to check the fridge. The guest last night had drank three cans of beer. I went out to my cart and brought in four. I put the three in the fridge then closed it and the closet doors. I pushed a chair up near the windows, undid the top button of my jacket and opened the beer.

I leaned forward my elbows on my knees and thought of all the summer days I had spent golfing in weather like this back home. I remembered the hot summer days fading into cool summer evenings which we spent drinking beer at a friend's cottage, watching

PART ONE

the moonlight wash onto the shore, lights on the other side of the inlet burning and flickering and dying in the darkness. In a way I desperately wanted to go home, but at the same time I knew that those days were gone, that my high school self didn't exist anymore, he was dead, a stranger looking out of a photograph whose face triggers a twinge of memory.

I was sitting there daydreaming, the door to the room wide open, when I heard an "ahem" behind me. I lowered my head expecting it to be Ferness, but the hand which touched my shoulder was Avi's.

"Peter, I know this is your last week, but…," he didn't seem to know but what, so he stopped and glanced at the closet. "The minibar is finished?" I nodded and he nodded back. "Drink your beer and let us go. Phipps is here."

"I know Phipps is here, I almost swore at him earlier."

"Peter, Mr. Phipps is…," he made a face and shook his hand in the air. "I hate him too, but you have to be careful. Let us go, we will have coffee in the kitchen."

I didn't answer. I took another drink and looked back out the windows. The grass seemed so close I felt I could touch it. I reached out and put the pads of my fingers on the glass. I pushed a little, I don't know what I expected, perhaps my life to begin.

Avi came up beside me and leaned against one of the wooden frames within the window, looking outside as well. He looked down at me and reached out his hand. I gave him the beer. He took a drink and gave it back.

"A few more days," he said, "then you can go out into the sunshine."

"Two weeks, then I will be back in school."

He nodded. "Well, life Peter."

The sun was on my face, silence all around us. The room felt incredibly still. Avi seemed to have lost all his concern about getting out of the room, lost in the warm air, the sunshine, pacing deep circles within himself.

"Avi, I know this is very personal, but I was…, well I'm curious about your wife."

FESTIVAL

Avi didn't look at me. He had his hands in his pockets, his gaze was dream-like out into the garden. Seconds passed. I leaned back in the chair thinking he wasn't going to answer.

"We had three years," he said. "Once at breakfast, only her and I at our little table, steam rising from my coffee, she said for two years she had been coming home to an empty house." He seemed to be telling a story that slightly puzzled him, the words coming slowly as though it was a story he had not thought of for a long time. "She said the warmth was gone from our blankets, there were no words in our books, no view from our windows. She said our love was gone."

He paused for a minute, and as he stood still beside me I noticed the absence of a cigarette, being so used to seeing Avi with smoke drifting around him. "I wasn't sad. I looked at the steam from my coffee, and when she finished she walked away but I was looking at the steam. I was thinking about the two years, they disappeared, they were not real anymore."

His voice drifted and died, the garden shone in the sunlight beyond the glass. I finished the beer and did up my top button. I stood up and my gaze focused on our faint reflections in the window. We looked like transparent ghosts. I tapped Avi and he turned, silent and handsome and polished in his dark red uniform, his glasses in one hand, the fingers of his right hand massaging his eyes. I followed him out into the hall and closed the door behind us.

༄

The late shift for the room attendant was three to ten, for the cook and porter it was three to eleven. If I was working the late shift with Toby we'd walk down to South Kensington together. Toby lived in Brixton. He transferred at Victoria and I kept going to Embankment to get a Charing Cross train to New Cross. The road from the Embankment station up to Charing Cross was always full of life. During the day there were people selling fruit, newspapers, an old homeless man who I bought the Big Issue from once in a while. At night there were always people walking around slightly drunk,

PART ONE

trying to get themselves home, and up by the McDonald's homeless guys lay in sleeping bags.

At the top of the street on the left a set of steps runs up inside Charing Cross station. At 11:00pm there are only a few scattered people standing around inside Charing Cross, the white light shining down as they stare up at the departure board, at the spinning numbers and spinning destinations and the electronic sign in the middle that either said nothing at all or apologized for mishaps. I would drift around until new destinations spun up on the board. When my train was announced I would step out to the tracks and trains and walk far out along my train until I was past the overhang of the station, open a door and step up into the deserted car, drop down beside the window and look out towards St. Paul's Cathedral.

The train runs across the river to Waterloo East, then runs to London Bridge. Buildings pass by that made me think of Dickens. They're old run down brick ghosts and I expected to see Bill Sykes slumped against one, bottle in his hand. All these battered depressed buildings shuffle past, but about three times, as though it is playing hide and seek, St. Paul's flashes through. It stands up into your vision its shoulders broad, looking white and ethereal but appearing so briefly, and so far away, beyond such wretches of battered architecture, that it almost becomes a mirage, something too good in which to believe. It teases you, it peeks its face between two brick shacks then disappears then flashes up again – and then St. Paul's leaves you.

You hit London Bridge and make the run to New Cross through the dark night with only the reflection of your face in the window. It always made me think of the chapter of *Sunshine Sketches of a Small Town* titled "L'Envoi." I was alone on the train, reality was slipping away, I was drifting back in time. Leacock said you can go home but your face will have changed in the city, your home won't know you.

My face would gaze thoughtfully at me from the window, and when I closed my eyes and leaned back against the seat I felt the train moving, heard the long suspended shush of the wheels and the whine of the metal tracks. I saw the ten year old Peter standing alone

FESTIVAL

in my old schoolyard, the wind pushing the trees back and forth in the night.

༄

TORONTO

If I was going to tell everything about Toronto, I'd say that four years ago it seemed so big I didn't think I'd ever be able to find my way around. But now I've spent my early twenties here, and Toronto has grown small for me. Little Falls remains *home*, but in some odd way that I'm unable to explain, Toronto has claimed me as well.

If I was going to explain Toronto I'd visit the city's outdoor hockey rinks in January and February, simply the sound of skates on ice, sticks slapping pucks and pucks hitting boards, voices and shouts and "I'm Open!" and open your eyes to see the rink's lights illuminating a sheet of ice and anywhere from five to twenty guys chasing a small black puck across frozen water, sticks in their hands, their grey breath wafting up above them through the glare of the lights and into the dark sky.

I'd go for a few more midnight walks down to the lake, pass through Christmas lights in Nathan Phillips Square at 2:00a.m., summer afternoons on Queen Street, the beaches in the east and the used bookstores in the Village in the west.

Shopping on Yonge Street at Christmas, homeless people freezing to death outside the World's Biggest Bookstore in the winter, the swarms of children in coloured jackets outside the ROM in the spring, the intersections you come to, like Spadina and College, when suddenly a canyon opens up heading south and you can see the CN Tower spearing the bright blue sky.

But explaining Toronto isn't what I'm trying to do here.

Let's go back to Sneaky Dee's.

In the morning and early afternoon it's the most beautiful place in Toronto. Debt ridden students, starving artists and tired musicians call friends, say "Do you want to meet for breakfast?" set a time then

PART ONE

head off without mentioning the location, but both go to Sneaky Dee's.

And it's never crowded.

You hang your red and black plaid jacket over a chair in the front alcove where windows border you on three sides, sit down in the sunlight, tap your fingers to the Miles Davis music and watch people circulate outside.

Someone pours you a cup of coffee, refills of which are free if they know you, and you order the $5.00 breakfast of eggs, bacon, toast and hashbrowns. While you're waiting you listen to four people at the table across from you debating minute details of Star Wars, and you slyly glance at the 30 year old skinhead in a heavy wool sweater who is reading the Globe's Arts and Entertainment section.

Flamenco Sketches is nearly over, the last track on the *Kind of Blue* album, and when your food is brought over and your coffee refilled you ask if they have any Gordon Lightfoot or Joni Mitchell.

Lightfoot's urgent acoustic guitar, Joni's sighing voice, either one and you're happy. The world is in motion outside those glass windows, cars and streetcars and bikes and pedestrians rattle and call and wave before disappearing around a corner, but you're still, even if it is only for half an hour. You have time to remember where you come from, to wonder where you're going, and you can sit in your chair as heavily as you want, you can rub the sleep out of your eyes as foolishly as possible, because everyone there is tired, everyone has stepped off the street to watch for a while.

When your cup is empty and your plate only bears a few tracks of egg yolk, you stand up, drop your Wilfrid Laurier $5.00 bill on the table with whatever coins you have in your pocket. You put your arms through the sleeves of your plaid jacket, nod or wave at the cook or server behind the bar, and step back out onto the sidewalk.

There's no snow but it's early winter and you aren't dressed warmly enough. You turn east with your collar up and your hands buried in your pockets. Gordon's voice is echoing in your mind: *Got my mail late last night, a letter from a girl who found the time to write.*

FESTIVAL

You walk past the fire station and clock tower, Massimo's the Spadina intersection, and you discover as you walk past these places that for each of them you have a store of memories. As you walk along you notice how natural Toronto feels under your feet, and you realize with a start that you aren't merely walking, you have a destination, you are going somewhere, and somewhere people are waiting for you.

PART TWO

How does it feel
To be on your own
With no direction home
Like a complete unknown
Like a rolling stone

Bob Dylan
Like a Rolling Stone

I woke to the falling rain, a voice gently gently beckoning me until I finally opened my eyes to shoo the whispering angel from my ear. I looked into Tracy's room, I checked the two rooms downstairs, but she had gone out somewhere. I made tea, added milk and sugar and sat in the living room holding the cup warm in my hands, watching the rain fall in Tracy's garden.

I packed. I folded myself into my backpack and sat looking around my room, contemplating carving my name into the wood of the bedpost as I carved my name into trees when I was a child.

The rain became a misty afterthought around lunch so I pulled my red pullover over a T Shirt and jeans and headed outside. I walked past Surrey Quays to Jamaica Road, crossed Tower Bridge and wandered west into the city following the river. I paused at Cleopatra's Needle which killed seven sailors while being dragged to England and which stands, amongst other things, on pictures of the most beautiful women in England at the time it was lifted into place.

I crossed under the Charing Cross bridge, past the Tattershall Castle Steamer, and stopped at the Air Force War Memorial. The Memorial is a golden eagle with its wings outstretched, sculpted in powerful flight, standing on top of a pillar inscribed with the motto "Upon the Wings of Eagles I Will Bear You Unto Me." Once earlier in the summer I was on the other side of the river, wandering around over there at night for some reason, and looking across at the Eagle I thought it was a sculpture of an angel with a glowing heart, descending to earth from the dark skies.

PART TWO

At Westminster Bridge, where Big Ben stood tall against the dark clouds, I put my hands on the wet ledge of the wall protecting me from the Thames. I had an hour to kill under a threatening sky.

By 4:00p.m. the sun had broken through the clouds above Knightsbridge. I was sitting on the curb across from the Benjamin waiting for Anne to pop her head up from the staff stairway. I stood when she appeared and crossed the street, the sun bright on the left side of her face, her right slightly in shadow, her long brown hair loose about her shoulders.

She stepped up onto the sidewalk with me. We moved together my hands in my pockets Anne wearing blue jeans and a grey T Shirt, her gold heart shaped locket dangling around her neck. We walked up Brompton Road past the Reject Shop, past the Bunch of Grapes and past Harrod's, where I looked around half-heartedly for Jen, her ghost, someone who smiled like her.

I heard my name tag a question but I wasn't sure what the question was, then Anne punched my shoulder. "Hey!"

"What?"

"Do you want to eat at a pub so that we can drink before we meet the others?"

"Sure."

She grinned. "Wake up Skywalker. It's your last day in London."

❦

At 6:00p.m. we crossed Charing Cross Road, passed the malnourished façade of the Hippodrome, walked along the narrow artery of shops and Greek/Italian diners that leads into Leicester Square, and on the edge of the Square I reached for Anne's hand and stopped her.

"Wait."

The open Square before us, humming with people, twilight in the glowing heart of London's nightlife.

"What?"

FESTIVAL

I shook my head and opened my palms emptily. "This."

Ringed by clubs and theatres and restaurants Leicester is the crossroads of the London night. Everyone celebrating life tonight would pass through the Square, and at this twilight hour you can feel the excitement building amongst the people swirling around you, in the shouts of the pizza makers, on the strings and in the horns of the scattered musicians, in the lights of the Odeon Cinema which dance brighter every second that the sun falls.

Anne and I moved into the Square, around the fence encircling the Leichester park. We spun through a wave of homeless women trying to jab flowers into our pockets, danced around a ring of tourists watching Jamaicans pounding steel carnival drums. In front of the Swiss Centre Anne held her hair and said "no no no" to hustler after hustler offering to tie her hair. We gambolled through a shower of barkers filling our hands with fliers and discounts and invitations to more clubs than we could have visited in an entire summer. We spun and danced and swirled amongst hundreds spinning and dancing and swirling.

Anne stepped into a crowd to watch a craftsman sitting on the pavement surrounded by leather and beads and baubles and metals making on the spot necklaces and jewellery. I swished my hand through her hair and ambled away to watch an artist working with chalk on the stones of the Square, a silky cushion beside him bearing coins, "Thank You" written underneath. Beside him stretched a gallery of artists, some of them with customers, tourists sitting to have their portraits drawn in pencil, most of the artists at leisure, reading magazines, watching people circle around them, the more industrious trying to make eye contact and draw in a customer.

I felt a hand touch and hold my shoulder. Turning I followed Anne through the crowd of ephemeral faces, the circling hum of passing bodies, the sound of night falling on an excited city.

The Buzz Bar sits on a side street at the southwest corner of Leicester. It occupies the ground and basement floors of a 5 or 6 storey building. The wall which faces the street is mainly glass,

PART TWO

looking across at a quiet movie theatre. Anne and I paid the cover at the front door and went inside, stopping to look around, acclimatize ourselves to the dim lighting and to the pop music they play so loud it makes your ribs vibrate.

The ground floor has a long L shaped bar on one side, booths along the walls and tables between the booths and the bar. The dance floor downstairs opens at 7:30 and from 5:30 to 7:30 is happy "hour" when you get a pint and a half for the price of a pint.

We wandered around for a few minutes, through the after work business people, the girls bouncing around in skintight skirts and jeans, until we saw Toby appear at the front door. Anne grabbed him and I went to the bar to buy the first round. I asked for three pints and a shot of Scotch, which I downed at the bar, carefully replacing the empty glass inside the ring of water from which I'd lifted it.

I put the three pints and three half pints on a tray and stood for a moment looking through the crowd for Anne and Toby. They were at one of the booths against the windows and picking up the tray I moved through the people and bodies to our table where I passed out the drinks. Toby clinked my glass saying "Cheers", Anne clinked and said "Here's looking at you kid," grinning at me, then we all took long drinks and brushed our fingers against our wet lips.

As I lowered my glass two hands clapped down on my shoulders and I heard my name shouted above me. Avi had appeared, beaming, Sarah and a girl I didn't know with him. I stood up, Sarah sat where I had been on the half circular bench around the table and Avi introduced me to Eva, who took my hand and said "Hello Peter, Avi told me about you." I smiled and said something utterly forgettable and Avi put his hand on my shoulder and pointed me towards the bar. "Are you drunk?" he shouted.

I stepped beside him and shook my head. "I've only had four pints over," I looked at my watch, "about two hours."

Avi spotted two empty bar stools and headed towards them, tapping people's shoulders and smiling politely to get by them. He waved at the bartender and ordered us two shots of Tequila and six pints of Fosters. As we waited, as the bartender worked the tap, Avi

FESTIVAL

pulled out a pack of cigarettes and a lighter. "You don't want one?" he said half jokingly and half out of common politeness.

I shook my head. "So Eva, she's the one you were talking about before, the one who can outdrink you?"

Avi smiled and nodded, sliding one of the Tequilas towards me. We lifted the glasses in the air and shot the drinks back. Avi set his glass down, turned to me with that gleam in his eyes which urged you to live a little and shouted my name again, the way he shouted everyone's name – Mulu, Ruth, Anne, Jennifer – as though he hadn't seen you for days and had been dying to talk to you. "One time I was here," he said, starting into one of his stories, "by myself after work, drinking right here," he tapped the bar where we were sitting with his right hand, his cigarette in his left hand. "I saw a woman, very very good looking, look at me. She was standing with some friends, she took a cigarette from one of them and walked to me, and she asked for a light."

The bartender began to place pints and half pints on the bar before us and Avi paused for a second to fish his wallet from his pocket and check his collection of notes. I touched my chest and pondered briefly what exactly it was in my chest that the music was making rattle.

"So we were talking and I said *Do you like to dance?* Then we were dancing for a long time and later on, on the dance floor, I asked her where her friends were, and she said they are gone." He leaned forward, smiling, putting his cigarette hand on his chest, "so I knew she was with me."

The bartender shouted a price at us over the bar, and Avi handed him some bills. I looked over my shoulder, trying to see Anne and the others through the bodies and noise of the bar. I caught a glimpse of Toby trying to look innocent while Anne laughed at him.

"So I took her home," Avi shouted, and I turned back to see him putting the change into his wallet. "And she was with me and at 4:00 in the morning," he shook four fingers at me, "Four! She said *I have to be at Heathrow in a few hours, I have to catch a plane* and she got out of bed and started getting dressed." Avi shook his head, smiling at the memory. "So I took her out and stood at the night bus stop with her and then she left."

He took a drink and looked at me awaiting a response. "Is that it?" I shouted.

"Yes."

"Why did you tell me that?"

"Elle est ici."

He was looking over my shoulder. I turned and saw a blond approach us, looking at Avi, holding an unlit cigarette in her hand. She stopped beside me, Avi reached his lighter out and flicked a flame to life.

"My name is Avi."

"Tina. How are you Avi?"

"I am well. Did you catch your plane?"

She nodded. "I catch lots of planes. I'm a flight attendant."

I looked from one to the other of them and wary of being a third wheel I grabbed my beer and stood up. "Please Tina take my chair. Avi…"

"I am coming with you." Avi stood up and smiled at Tina. "I am sorry but I am with friends tonight." He shrugged his shoulders and Tina nodded. "Well it was nice meeting you anyway," she said. "Take care."

"You also."

She turned and left us. Avi put out his cigarette and picked up three of our six pints. "Stay here, I will send Sarah and Anne for the half pints." I nodded and watched Avi weave like a professional waiter through the people between the bar and the booth where the others were sitting. I picked up and gulped down one of the half pints, watching Anne and Sarah rise and move towards me. When they arrived I picked up the pints, they grabbed the half pints and we wagon-trained back to the table.

Toby and Avi ended up in the middle of the half circle, with Eva and then me on Avi's side, and Anne then Sarah on Toby's side, Sarah and I on the two ends of the bench. Sarah was wearing a sleeveless black dress that just touched to her knees, her dark brown hair loose in waves falling over her shoulders. Eva was wearing brown jeans and an oatmeal coloured top with long sleeves and buttons which began below her breasts and ran up to her neck. Eva was taller than me, with a strong Germanic appearance. As we talked, as the night went on and we joked and laughed around the table, shouting at each other to make ourselves heard over the music, I found that Eva landed halfway between being one of the boys and being very sexily feminine. She could do both – she could take a swig of her pint and crack a joke or she could nudge Avi and cast him a look which made me feel cold simply because I wasn't part of it. It made me wonder what Inga was like – Avi's other girlfriend who had sent her friend Eva to Avi. What would happen when these two friends came face to face again with Avi between them? Could Avi truly be happy letting them decide who he would stay with?

But all that would happen after I left, and I tried to put it out of my mind, concentrating on little things – the way Avi and Toby exhaled plumes of smoke into the air, the goofy faces of people who stopped as they were passing outside to crane and peer through the windows, the way the girls seemed to use ESP to all head off to the washroom at the same time, and the way Anne grinned and Sarah and Eva laughed when they returned and Toby and Avi and I left for the washroom.

We bought a few more rounds, I made periodic trips to grab a shot of something, the seating arrangement changed and eventually I found myself staring at Sarah's palm, unsure of why her hand was in mine or why the girls were looking at me expectantly.

I looked from one to the other of them, catching a grin in Anne's eye as she realized that I was drunk and didn't know what was going on. "So what about these gypsies?" she asked.

I stared at her for a few seconds, still holding Sarah's hand in mine. "Was I talking about gypsies?"

"The gypsies from your hometown who taught you to read palms," Sarah said.

PART TWO

I looked at Sarah, then down at her palm. "You want your palm read?"

Sarah shrugged her shoulders. "You said it wouldn't be too hard."

I nodded and turned from her eyes, running my thumb over the faint lines of her wrist, down through the valley of her hand to her soft white fingers. I had done this before, once at university I had found myself encircled by girls at a bar after being dared to pick someone and ask her if she wanted her palm read. I had been drunk that time as well.

"So Sarah," I said, "what is it you are interested in?"

"Whatever you can see."

I pressed my thumb into the centre of her palm for a few seconds and then looked up into her eyes. "A sunny garden, a sun hat, a wooden fence behind you. You're reading a book."

"Maybe."

"You've just put your book down to grab your grey and white kitten who's been jumping around batting at butterflies and moths."

Excited, Sarah closed her fingers and grasped my hand in hers. "That was my house in Oxford where I grew up!"

"You were a cute kid."

"What about the future?"

"Who cares about the future?"

She squeezed my hand harder. "I do!"

"Yeah, but…"

"Please Peter, who will my great love be?"

I took a drink of beer and looked past Sarah through the glass at the street. I didn't want to do this anymore. I didn't know how to read palms and Sarah was too nice a person to lie to like this. I shook my head and looked down at her hand, the centre of a tiny pool of quiet within the clamour and noise and bustle of the Buzz Bar.

"Your husband will be someone you have already met, someone that within two years you'll be spending a lot of time with, but not in London. I guess that means you'll be going back to Oxford. I think his name is Roger or Robbie. Either of those sound familiar?"

Sarah pursed her lips. "Robert?"

"Ah, Robert. That's good. What is he, a veterinarian or a dentist or something?"

"The last I heard he worked halftime with British Rail."

I let Sarah's hand go and reached for my beer. "British Rail, I should have guessed that, your loveline feels like a railroad track. I was wondering what that meant."

Anne muttered "Oh Boze" and clapped her hand to her forehead.

"What's the matter with you?"

"Your bull is giving me a headache."

"Oh ye of little faith."

"Look who's talking."

"Why don't you try?" Sarah said.

Anne offered me her hand. I smiled and finished a half pint. I touched my fingers to hers and bending my head down kissed the palm of her hand. "You're going to develop a fetish for Elvis toothbrushes."

"You're late. I already went through that phase."

"Anne I don't want to do this anymore."

"What about love?"

"I don't deal with love."

"You told Sarah about getting married."

"I was lying and this became stupid several minutes ago."

"Well tell me something Pizzaman."

"You had a Sylvester the Cat doll when you were young." The grin on her face faded, her eyes widened in astonishment. "You used to walk around the schoolyard saying *Hey do you want to play Sylvester?* And none of the kids knew what you meant, so you'd say *That's where you say Aaaaaaahh Shut Up! And hit me once then I grab you and hit you about 20 times!*"

Anne punched my shoulder. Hard. "I must have told you that!" she shouted.

"No."

"So what about my future?"

I looked into her eyes for a few seconds, then down at her palm. I lifted my other hand and pressed her hand between mine, our palms together. For a while that was all I was aware of, our hands suspended together above a wooden surface, a warm intimate handshake, and then the scope of my vision enlarged. I saw my arms and Anne's arms, and then Anne and all the glasses on the table, then Sarah and Toby and Avi and Eva at the table, and releasing her hand and sitting back on the bench I smiled at her. "I can't."

"Why?"

"The past is the only thing that's real. It's the only thing that doesn't change."

"So you aren't going to predict my future?"

"Only if you want me to make something up?"

"It's that difficult?"

I nodded and looked around to see if one of the beers was obviously mine. I grabbed a full pint and downed a quarter of it. "The future's brutal."

Anne regarded me quietly for a few seconds, then leaned back in her seat and glanced at Avi, who leaned forward over the table. "You are finished Peter?" he asked. I shrugged and Avi nodded. "We can finish our drinks and then go downstairs, the dance floor is open now."

Anne glanced at her watch and then looked across the table at Sarah who took a tentative and careful sip from one of the full half pints. Eva, Toby, Avi and I were quiet for about a minute, taking long slugs of our beers until we only had a few glasses to carry downstairs to the dance floor. The others began to rise and I stepped away from the table, the movement giving me a disorienting buzz and I staggered slightly then grabbed the side of the table, shaking my head to clear away the dizziness.

The Buzz Bar has two floors. The main floor has the bar and the tables, and is the one you walk in on from the street. The downstairs floor is closed until 7:30pm when the DJ cranks up and the dancing officially begins. You go downstairs via a wide swirling wooden staircase that empties into the neutral area between the dance floor and the downstairs bar. For a moment we were all together at our table upstairs, me holding onto the table for support, the others

FESTIVAL

milling around, picking up glasses, straightening shirts and dresses. Then Toby moved off towards the staircase, Avi patted my shoulder and smiled as he and Eva went after Toby, then Anne and Sarah beside me, turning me towards the staircase.

The dance floor is the size of a large swimming pool, sitting about half a metre below the rest of the downstairs floor, the DJ booth on a raised stage at one end. At the bottom of the stairs Avi and Eva turned right towards the bar and Toby, Sarah, Anne and I turned left to the dance floor – the mass of moving bodies.

I was the last one. First Toby and Sarah pushed their way in, then Anne, then I added into the crowd as I had once entered the Gulf of Mexico – tentative, unsure of where I was stepping, clearing a path before me, leaving a momentary ripple of a wake that was immediately brushed over as bodies reclaimed their space behind me.

I remember spurious glimpses of Toby, a face set in concentration revealed once in a while through jolting heads and flying hands, and Sarah, dancing beautifully, illuminated once in a spotlight, her arms raised above her head her eyes closed – my last image of her.

Anne was around longer, my eyes would clear and I'd see her light brown hair flying through the air, her mischievous grin, but even Anne faded away.

In London, in the basement of the Buzz Bar, I floated through pounding electronic tribal music, a woman chanting "Buzzzz Barrrr" above a sea of dancers, flying elbows, strange girls who appeared to grind their hips against my thighs before disappearing into the sea of pulsating mindless bodies.

I entered a world where music over loaded my hearing, constant contact overloaded my sense of touch, the odour of sweat drowned all smells, the alcohol deadened my mouth and the darkness rendered me blind, leaving me alone.

And then the smoke.

Periodically misty tendrils rose from the corners of the dance floor. The dancing would slow, the smoke seeping towards you, people waving goodbye to partners as the smoke gives its final embrace. You are blind, the world is grey, you can sense nothing but the brutish thumps of drums which shake your ribs. Occasional arms and elbows reach from their world into yours, striking your body, but they disappear back into the mist, leaving only a memory of pain to mark the brief encounter.

When the smoke fades the dancing intensifies, faces are revealed, looks cast, bodies touched. You step off the dance floor where people stand drinking and you're watching – you see the dj in her cage, the sea of heads, hear the feet stamp and the music pound, close your eyes and hear the feet pound, feel the smoke build.

&

I was on the Strand. I was walking, hurrying. I felt an arm linked through mine. Anne.

&

I was in Trafalgar Square. Anne beside me, rolling her jeans up over her knees. Her face was bright, laughing. She stood up straight, looking at me. "What are you waiting for? Did you change your mind?"

"About what?"

"You said you wanted to run through the fountains."

I looked at the fountains – they weren't fountaining. No water was running, the whole Square was silent. I couldn't see anyone save Anne and I..., no, there was one other. He was sitting on a lion under Nelson's column, his eyes sad, dressed as though waiting to step out into a Checkov winter.

I turned to Anne and started rolling up my jeans. Anne moved to the fountain and stepped up onto the wide edge then into the pool, wading towards the center, placing her hands on the higher bowl trying to peer inside. I felt ten years old, Anne and I should have been children together.

I stepped up into the water, not believing how blue it was. I could see coins at my feet. Where was the light coming from? I

FESTIVAL

stopped at a silver coin and reached into the water. It was a Canadian dime. I found a five pence piece, a U.S. quarter. I knelt low to the water, opened my hand and watched them drift down into the blue.

We jumped out and ran across the Square through the vague after midnight darkness to the other pool, wading carefully, trying to avoid splashing water above our knees, trying to keep our jeans dry.

A shout came from somewhere, voices creeping in. An albatross came running towards our pool, chest bare, jumping, banging one knee on the stone and falling clumsily into the water. He stood grasping his knee, shouting to a friend who approached from the wall on the north of the Square. "My knee! You poxy bastard Len, don't laugh!"

I was aghast. I looked up into the night sky to see where he'd fallen from. I thought I was dreaming again.

Anne was no longer in the pool. I saw her back at the first one, a grey figure in the darkness, struggling with her pant legs.

I stepped out of the water and onto the side of the pool. The drunk albatross was splashing around. He sent water my way as I stepped down onto the stones of the Square. I put my hands in my pockets, my pants legs still rolled up. I glanced at the sad little child as he watched me cross the stones.

I sat down on the edge of Anne's pool. She had her legs stretched out trying to unroll her jeans which had tightened around her knees.

"Could you use some help?"

She nodded, her face almost in a grimace as she tried to push her jeans down her legs. We were alone again. The albatross was in the other pool but I had tuned him out. I could sense Nelson in the sky, unseen and impotent but still there. I could sense the boy on the lion looking down at me. The sky was black, the moon hidden by unseen clouds but the Square was lit, as though a nightlight had been turned on somewhere.

I put my hands on the cuff of Anne's right pant leg and pulled. It took forever but slowly it came loose, then we worked the other one down. I stood up and pushed my own pant legs down, stepped back into my shoes.

"Anne how did we get here?"

She was on the edge of the pool, her feet dangling down towards the Square as you dangle your legs over the edge of a dock. "We walked."

"Where are Avi and Toby and Sarah?"

"You don't remember?"

"No."

"Well, they just kind of went their way. We left Avi and Eva at the bar, Toby went to Charing Cross, Sarah left us when we went into KFC." Anne looked at me with a sly grin on her face. "Sarah invited you to go home with her."

"Oh yeah? What'd I say?"

"You said *I'm smarter than the average bear.*"

I laughed and rubbed my fingertips into my tired eyes.

"What do you want to do now?"

I turned to Nelson's Column, the little wraith sitting on the lion, the eyes from the past which were so sad. I reached my hand towards Anne. She laced her fingers through mine and moved with me over the stones, through the silence and darkness, to Nelson's Column. The boy slid down off the lion, pattering down into the Square as we stepped up onto the base level where the four lions lie.

I gazed out past the Square, at the cars and buses circling us, St. Martin's Lane running up past St. Martin's in the Fields, the National Gallery a squat solid shadow in the greater darkness, my pants slightly damp against my skin, the smell of stagnant water telling me to say goodbye and move on.

"Peter."

I turned to Anne who was sitting on the first gradation above the level of the lions. She nodded her head towards a guy who was moving towards us. He was in his mid twenties wearing jeans and a plaid shirt. He had a joint in his hand. He held it out to us. "You two smoke?"

I murmured "no." Anne beamed and fell from her sitting position. She moved to him saying "thanks!" and took the joint from his hand.

FESTIVAL

He said "keep it" and wandered back to the southeast lion where another guy was sitting, gazing down Northumberland Avenue towards the Thames.

Anne dragged on the joint a few times, holding the smoke down inside her lungs before letting it go. "You really don't want any?" she asked, her voice hoarse.

I shook my head. "I'm going to talk to those guys," she said, and she moved down towards them. I stepped backwards and leaned against my lion, a bemused participant in a fairy tale.

"Thanks."

"Yeah."

"You guys ever do BT's?"

Silence. "Wot? Like the telephone?"

"No!" and Anne's laugh. "Bottle Tokes!"

The two guys exchanged confused looks and I turned away, moving around my lion so that I was standing on the edge of the column step, looking directly at the National Gallery.

In the Square, between the fountains, the boy was playing hopscotch. A clown appeared, of grey smoke, pantomiming an act for him. I jumped up onto the lion, my feet on his foreshoulders, then balancing carefully I stood on his head. The boy had stopped playing, his fingers on his lips in suppressed joy, watching the clown fumble through an ancient dance.

"You put a little hole in the bottom of a beer bottle, put the hash on the lit end of a cigarette, stick it in the hole..." then Anne's voice faded away.

I saw ghostly figures appearing from every recess of night. A ringmaster appeared in the center of the Square, directing seals on beach balls, bears on leashes lions in cages acrobats climbing rope ladders to the trapeze that hung ethereal in the sky. I couldn't hear the ringmaster. I couldn't hear anything, silence as heavy as the night enveloped me.

Grey wraiths were floating, dancing, juggling, ghostly silent lions came to life, roaring emptily at their trainer fending them off with a chair. A ferris wheel, sitting on the elevated northern part

PART TWO

of the Square, began churning silently, filling the sky, the National Gallery only a dark mass beyond, like the groups of trees that appear as dinosaurs beside the highway on raining midnight trips through the Ontario countryside.

A trapeze act, a ghost with clenched feet inching along a high wire, flying gymnasts hanging upside down from the swinging trapeze bars, their arcs moving them away and towards each other. A woman hung from one gymnast's arms, as the arcs began to greet each other grips tightened then released, fingers breaking from wrists to suddenly be grasping nothing but night sky, the woman somersaulting, the ghost who had released her briefly following, the ghost who would catch her approaching, arms outstretched, head bent back, hands reaching for hands, compressing the night between their fingers stretching stretching until a violent clap locked fingers onto wrists and the arc swung them back up into the night.

It was a festival of silent ghosts, the Square teeming with grey ethereal bodies, the ferris wheel spinning, bears on hind legs rampaging, the ringmaster at center stage the little boy sitting on the edge of a pool and with him a gallery – friends from childhood birthday parties who would gather around my cake in the kitchen while I hid under my bed refusing to take part, friends from highschool and university, my parents, Hannah and Daniel, my friend who I tipped a canoe with in the middle of a lake during a windstorm, a friend at university pouring a bottle of wine over my head as we danced, another friend coming up to me saying "God Peter are you ever sweating!" and the girl who had poured the wine shouting gleefully "That's not sweat! I poured a bottle of wine on him!"

So many people, so many different Peters – how had I known them all and how do we hold onto it all?

I stood on Nelson's Column eyes wide unable to take it all in. It was Carnival in Orleans it was Festival in Rio it was the bright lights of Leichester Square and the life of Covent Gardens. It was everything I had ever been.

The trapeze appeared again. A man swinging towards me, head back arms outstretched, reaching for me as he had reached for the

FESTIVAL

woman. I shifted my weight forward onto my toes, I began leaning forward, lifting my arms, stretching them towards the smiling, assuring ghostly face and smoky hands that were swinging towards me.

Slowly, so slowly that I had time to see a child run across a river, a boy fly high into the sunlight, another boy cold in a midnight thunderstorm, the acrobat reached the end of his arc, coming as close to me as possible. I reached for the hands, expecting to catch hold and be swung out onto the trapeze, above the festival through the darkness, a child smiling at the feel of the wind in his hair, at the delight of gravity emptying out of his body.

The smoky fingers began to fade, curling away in wafts of Avi's cigarette smoke, wisps of grey in the darkness. The hands, wrists, arms and smile all faded, an empty trapeze bar swung away from me, fading as it swung back. The clown turned to smoke, the lions and elephants, the ferris wheel, my sad eyed friend, the gallery of my past and present, face after face until finally I was left alone.

I stood on my lion watching the smoke thin and rise, leaving cold stones and two dark silent fountains. I felt a familiar emptiness within me, the desire again to press an anvil into my chest to satisfy my heart's demand for substance.

I sat down on the lion's back, my legs stretching down his side. I watched lone figures cross the stones before me, the headlights of cars and buses circle the Square, dark clouds roll overhead, the flag outside my embassy flutter quietly in the night.

I covered my eyes – alone in Trafalgar Square, in London which echoed with the sounds of midnight life and where I sat silent on a stone lion – tired of building sandcastles at the water's edge, tired perhaps of simply being alive.

*

I was on a bus. My face in the window. Shapes passed in the darkness, streetlights approaching then disappearing. Anne's voice, a whisper tugging the sleeve of my mind. "This is your last night in London."

PART TWO

I turned to her from the window, discovering that I could see the reflection of my face in her eyes.

❦

Anne's arms. Her face before me, smiling, her long hair sweeping gently towards her mouth.

She kissed my lips, she kissed the small birthmark on my nose. She kissed the dream I'd had as a child of the rose burning in the night.

She was below me. My lips on hers, my hand on her bare stomach, her hands on my shoulders, but also a mist, and I couldn't see her. I could feel her body, hear her voice, but she was lost in a fog.

I lifted my head and waved my hand before my face.

"What are you doing?"

A voice out of the night. I lifted myself to my knees and doing so fell of the bed. Through the mist I could hear movement, the settling of bed springs.

❦

I was standing at the foot of the bed, stepping into my shoes. Anne was sitting cross-legged amongst the sheets, her face barely visible through the gloom. "Don't you have anything to say about what we just did?"

"You're welcome?"

"You're such a stupid bastard."

"I'm not going to say I love you."

A pillow struck my head. I picked it up and lightly tossed it back to Anne. I tapped my fingers on the bedframe. I moved around to sit in the chair between the bed and the window, looking at the streetlight outside, the moon and stars hidden by clouds. The streetlight cast a pool of light across the room, from my feet past Anne's bed towards the door. I tapped my heels together, thinking of pixie dust and Judy Garland – tapping my heels together, ready in a few hours to fly away.

FESTIVAL

∽

A cup of tea in her hands, sitting on the bed, her feet up on the chair I had vacated. My hands in my pockets as I stood before the window.

"Can I ask you about home?"

Her breath across tea. "What about it?"

I looked at the dark quiet street, drops of water on the window heralding rain. "When I go back to my parents' house, my hometown, it's to visit a world of memories rather than touch real life again. Without my knowing it the place I've always thought of as home has been steadily disappearing. You've been gone longer than I have, I'm wondering what you call home."

Anne in grey light on the bed, blowing steam from her tea. "I don't know Peter," she whispered, her voice drifting across the room like a toy sailboat, floating slowly over becalmed water. "*Peter*. Wow, I just realized that I'm going to miss saying your name."

I didn't answer. She ran a hand along the bed, smoothing, straightening wrinkles in the darkness. "Home is fairly illusive. I guess for me it's the next city or person or job I fall in love with. I mentally hang up my hat and say *Well here I am so this must be home!*"

I looked down at the floor. Anne took a sip of tea and the echo of sound floated quietly across to me.

"Do you know who Paul Theroux is?" she asked.

"He's a travel writer."

"He has a saying, or he picked up a saying from some tribe – *always remember, wherever you go, there you are.*"

∽

"Anne?"

Silence. Raindrops touching the window. I could picture her behind me holding her teacup in both hands.

"That Rothko you stood me in front of destroyed me."

Silence again. Rain.

PART TWO

"I knew that when the summer was over I'd be saying goodbye to you, to Avi, the life I'd created here. Another goodbye on top of all the others, and my goodbyes aren't balanced by anything. I go through life looking for endings, and when life gives me beginnings I turn them over in my hands until I've found out how they end. That Rothko makes you live within your own emotions, and mine all concern loss."

"Have you ever asked yourself why?"

"Isn't loss a fundamental truth?"

"So is gain. It's a two sided coin."

❦

My hand on the bedpost, my body facing the door, ready to allow the valley to form – the valley between past and present, the real and spirit worlds.

"Peter," she said, her voice like a hand on my shoulder. "I know you're leaving and I'm not asking you this because I'm trying to stop you…"

"What are you asking me?"

"What is it you feel for me?"

I turned and gazed at her as though I hadn't heard the question, as though it was still floating through the darkness between us, me waiting for the butterfly of sound to touch my forehead. "What do you mean?"

"It's a simple enough question Alfalfa."

"Not for everyone." I moved around and sat down on the bed, facing Anne standing by the window, a dull aura of light softening the edges of her waist and arms and neck and hair. I started speaking without looking at her, staring at the floor between my feet. "Avi asked me once if you and I were together. I said no and he was surprised. I think a little disappointed as well."

"Why?"

"I don't know." I rubbed my hands together, remembering the surprised look on Avi's face at Le Petit Prince. "Avi and I are very

119

different people. He's much more alive than I am. When he's given the opportunity for intimacy with someone he opens the doors wide and welcomes it with a smiling face. I circle opportunities to take a look from behind and see what is being hidden. I circle everything."

"You've circled my question."

I looked at her, trying to remember, and remembering looked down at her feet, my elbows on my legs, my hands clasped together between my knees. "Anne I'm not terribly sure if it is possible for me to love."

I had expected a laugh and a rebuttal but none came. I looked up at her in front of the window, the light behind her, a recreation of the shadowy picture I'd taken of her in the Mall. "As I sit here talking to you I'm glad that I can talk to you, I'm glad that you're listening, I'm grateful for our friendship, but love implies permanence..."

"And tomorrow you're flying away."

"I'm always flying away." I looked at her, trying to find her face through the shadows. "I hate my life Anne. Every year I find a new room to stick my mattress and desk in and I find a few new friends that I know I'll eventually be saying goodbye to. It's like having my teeth pulled by a sadist. It's like we're all ghosts, unable to reach out and take another ghost by the hand."

I stood and moved to the window beside Anne. I put my fingers on the glass. "Last summer a friend of mine, who's only a year older than me, got married. Privately we were all saying things like *I can't believe he's getting married, he's too young, kiss of death*, but ever since the ceremony I've been thinking of how beautiful marriage is. You put a ring on a ghost's finger and he or she becomes flesh and blood, one real person that you can hold onto. My parents have that, my sister has that, my friend has that, and I guess that's love and I guess love is real, but there are two sides to love. Look at Avi, my landlady, even you and I tonight – everything is destined to end and it seems pointless to bother fighting that.

"But then I know that it's not pointless. If I had a younger brother I'd tell him to fill his life with every friend and love and happiness that he could get his hands on, but I've been too afraid of

PART TWO

love dying, of life ending, to take that advice." I paused, my fingertips searching the window, trying to touch the drops of rain on the other side of the glass. "I want a guarantee of permanence. I don't want to build my life amongst ghosts."

Anne stood before me in the darkness, measuring me, half her face illuminated by the streetlight outside, the other half in shadow, and for the first time I noticed the shade of grey in the blue iris of her right eye. She stood gazing at me for several seconds, and as I broke the gaze to look across the dark room at the door she stepped into me, an arm around me, her head on my shoulder, her breasts against my chest, her left hand weaving itself into my right, fingers interlocking, securing something between our palms.

For a long time I stood in her arms like a statue, looking through the window at the street I'd soon be walking on, the rain which would be falling on me, then gradually I noticed the scent of her perfume, a sensation of warmth beginning in our clasped hands, and as I hesitantly began to brush my fingers against hers she whispered "I'm real."

I watched a few last raindrops touch the window, then closed my eyes, lowering my face into the silkiness of her hair.

꩜

The door closed behind me. I moved down the walk to the gate, through the gate onto the sidewalk. I paused for a second, unsure of which way to turn. Black buildings shouldered a silent street that seemed to lead nowhere in two directions.

I turned left and stepped into a pool of still water. I abandoned the sidewalk and walked down the middle of the deserted street, through a patch of light thrown by a streetlight into darkness, then light then darkness, then light…

꩜

FESTIVAL

I made it to New Cross by 6:30a.m. Tracy woke around 8:00 and made me eggy bread for breakfast. I swung my backpack onto my shoulders, Tracy kissed my cheek and said "farewell" then closed the door behind me. I took my last ride on the London Underground.

I arrived at Heathrow with an hour and a half to kill before my plane boarded. I wandered around, past the Thomas Cooks, the aisles of airport chairs holding people who were sleeping or reading or staring into space. I stopped at one of the arrival areas and saw a father and daughter standing amidst a crowd waiting for passengers to begin filing through the gate.

They were young. The daughter was around five and he must have been around thirty. They were playing a game. He would put his hands under her arms and she would start pedalling her legs as though riding a bike, laughing as her father lifted her and she pedalled herself into the air.

I stepped away across the terminal and waited, and eventually the mother appeared, a youngish girl next door woman, picking up the girl and hugging her, the father's arms around them both. I picked up my backpack and walked away.

I presented my ticket, smiled at the stewardess at the door and sat down beside a girl who turned out to be the friend of a friend and lived in a building in Toronto that I walked by several times a week during school.

The seatbelt sign came on, the plane taxied away and I put my hands over my eyes. The friend of a friend asked if I was afraid of flying.

EPILOGUE

December 11

Anne:

Last night when I was walking home from work at 11:00pm it was snowing, really snowing - the type of thick white packable snow that drives children crazy on Christmas mornings.

The streets were deserted, no snow plows were on the roads there were hardly any cars, every street I turned onto was a straightaway of soft pure angelic snow, and all around me, filling the air as in a dream, snowflakes were falling, setting in my hair in my palms on my tongue.

The first thing I did was throw a couple of snowballs at telephone poles, then I started running and sliding, then I ran and dove, then I just kept running.

I ran all the way home along College, grabbed my roommates, made them put on their winter boots and coats and run with me to grab three of our friends who have an apartment on the way to school, and at school we grabbed all the girls we knew who are still in residence.

We ran around our college quadrangle making snowangels, having snowball fights, then a veritable army from another college came through and started throwing snowballs at us, people emptied out of the residences which ring our Quad and a snowball war began.

I found myself laughing when I was getting a face wash by two of the friends that I'd collected. I got up and chased Oscar down but just when I was getting him back the two of us started getting pelted

EPILOGUE

by some of the girls we'd brought out with us. I tackled one, Oscar tackled another and the third got away, but came back trying to over power Oscar who was having so much fun that all he could do was lie on his back and laugh and kick his legs while the two of them stuffed snow inside his shirt and down the back of his pants.

I stood up eventually and helped my friend Karen off the ground, smiling away the jokingly revengeful look that she gave me. I watched Oscar rolling on the ground laughing, yelling "Help me Peter!" while trying to escape the girls who were covering him in snow.

I watched Tyler and Steve rolling a snowball towards the bottom two thirds of a snowman, in the widening distance behind them people were running and diving, snowballs flying.

The old Victorian buildings of the College loomed as high shadows around the Quad, the branches of trees caught snow, creating a spread of gleaming white spiderwebs, and out of the sky, out of the darkness, snowflakes kept falling, entering the glow of the quad as a swirl of heavenly dust, a flurry of rice and confetti at a wedding.

I stood amidst this wintry festival for a long time until I noticed Karen beside me, bent at the waist, brushing snow off her pants with her mitts. I said "Hey!" and when she stood straight to see what I wanted I put my arms around her and hugged her. "It's Christmas," I said. "This is a Christmas hug."

She put her arms around me and kissed me on the cheek. She looked into my eyes, trying to be serious, trying to jokingly scold me for wrestling her into the snow, but her cheeks were red her hair was wet and seeing that she was trying to keep from laughing I started laughing. She put her wet mitts on my cheeks her face bright and she whispered "Merry Christmas."

I'm not going to say that I wish it was you rather than Karen that I hugged last night, but I will say that I wish I had hugged you like that in London, hugged you because I felt happy, because I felt alive.

FESTIVAL

Today is one of my days off Anne. It's early morning. I'm sitting on the couch in our TV room, drinking tea, watching the sunlight break outside, and when I lift my pen from this letter I'm going to step out into that sunlight, find a post office box and send paper bound words to do what I wish I could do in person – step up to you with a grin on my face, mistletoe in my hand, glad tidings in my arms.

I can't hug you but let me do what I can, and do it while feeling happy, feeling alive

Merry Christmas, Anne.

Peter
Toronto